T0126003

Short Dog

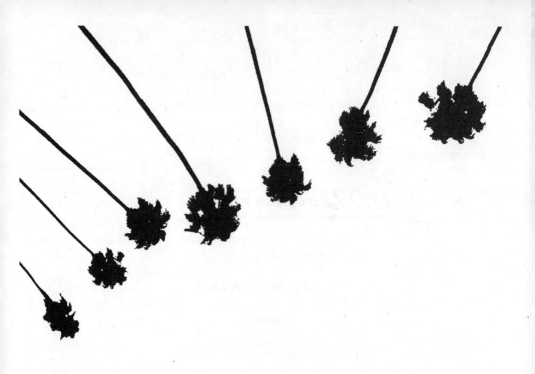

BLACK SPARROW PRESS • Boston • 2021

Short Dog

CAB DRIVER STORIES FROM THE L.A. STREETS

DAN FANTE

With an introduction by
WILLY VLAUTIN

Published in 2021 by **BLACK SPARROW PRESS**

GODINE
Boston, Massachusetts
www.godine.com

The publisher would like to thank *Beat Scene* and Bottle of Smoke Press, where
some of these stories first appeared.

LIBRARY OF CONGRESS CATALOGING-IN-PUBLICATION DATA
Names: Fante, Dan, 1944- author.
Title: Short dog : cab driver stories from the L.A. streets / Dan Fante.
Description: Boston : Black Sparrow Press, 2021.
Identifiers:
LCCN 2020042606 (print)
LCCN 2020042607 (ebook)
ISBN 9781574232493 (paperback)
ISBN 9781574232509 (ebook)
Subjects: LCSH: Taxicab drivers--Fiction. | Los Angeles (Calif.)--Fiction.
   | LCGFT: Short stories.
Classification: LCC PS3556.A545 S56 2021 (print) | LCC PS3556.A545
   (ebook) | DDC 813/.54--dc23
LC record available at https://lccn.loc.gov/2020042606
LC ebook record available at https://lccn.loc.gov/2020042607

Cover Design: Alex Camlin

FIRST PRINTING, 2021
Printed in Canada

For Ayrin Leigh Fante &
Michelangelo Giovanni Fante
With every beat of my heart

And for my father, John Fante
Thank you, you magnificent son of a bitch!

Contents

Bangin' Out the Dents

AN INTRODUCTION BY WILLY VLAUTIN

I MET DAN FANTE AT a restaurant in Paris. He was short
and burly and wore these black James Joyce glasses and
he grinned at me while chewing Nicorette gum like his life
depended on it. We sat next to each other and became instant
friends because we both knew that we had stumbled into a run
of luck. We were staying at an upscale hotel paid for by our
French publisher and we were eating like kings. I think we were
both so surprised by the situation that it felt like we'd pulled off
a heist and had somehow gotten away with it. So, everything on
that trip seemed a laugh, an easy time, and a gift, because we
both had a lot of miles behind us where you wouldn't have bet
even a cent that we'd end up working writers in a foreign coun-
try meeting each other in a fancy restaurant.

I'd read *86'd* and *Chump Change* and loved his alter ego,
Bruno Dante, but I didn't know anything about Dan Fante
before that night in Paris except that his father was the
famous writer John Fante. Many people know that Dan had
a tattoo on his right arm for his brother that read NICK FANTE,
DEAD FROM ALCOHOL, 1-31-42 TO 2-21-91. I didn't, and that night
I couldn't stop looking at it. I also didn't know that Dan was
an old-school AA guy with decades of sobriety under him
and a wisdom and ease in talking about it. When he caught

me staring at the tattoo, he told me about his brother's, his father's, and his own struggles with alcohol. I told him about my struggle and my brother's. He was so warm and generous with his life wrecks, near wrecks, losses, and occasional wins that when I left that night I called my brother, who was just waking up in Los Angeles, and told him about Dan because he was the first writer I'd ever met who seemed truly grateful for and surprised by the success he'd had. He was also the first writer I'd met who made me feel normal.

Dan had his family with him, his wife and young son, and with our publisher we spent a week traveling around France doing readings and promoting our novels and never once did the goddamn-I'm-lucky-to-be-here feeling leave either of us. We said goodbye after our final event and went our own ways, only to find ourselves in the same railcar the next morning. He came back to where I was and sat next to me and said, "We're in a rough racket, huh?" Yeah, I told him. "I don't know how much longer I'm gonna be around so I gotta write something that sells for my son. That's what I'm going to do next." He chewed his Nicorette and looked out the window and then looked back at me. "But we got lucky on this run, huh?"

Maybe that he survived books like *Chump Change, Mooch, Spitting Off Tall Buildings, 86'd*, and the collection here, *Short Dog: Cab Driver Stories from the L.A. Streets*, was why he was so at peace when I met him. Because the stories you're about to read are those of a cab driver on the edge of madness. Bruno Dante is a struggling writer living near the bottom. A place where success is met with a self-inflicted defeat to keep you there. As he says in the story "Mae West": "Everything I touched seemed to be turning to pain." As Bruno drives dilapidated cabs around Los Angeles, we meet Wifebeater Bob, the alcoholic doorman; Bernie, the musician who knows how to beat Antabuse; Leslee, the massage therapist; Libby and Bitch, the drug addled Hollywood-ites and their Burmese python, Princess; THEBOBBY, a wannabe actor who robs his drunk fares; and the heartbreaking insanity of Missus Randolph and her daughter.

Short Dog is a collection soaked in booze and sadness, psychotic eruptions and hilarity. When I finished the book the first time, it felt like passing out drunk in a sleeping bag in a vacant lot only to be awoken from a fever dream under the midday sun, hungover and sweating and unable to get the bag unzipped: glad to be alive and desperately in need of a drink. But now when I look back at this collection, I think of survival. Maybe if you hang on long enough and try your best to bang out the dents in yourself, you might escape the short dog and the madness it gives and you might have, at least for a bit, an easy run.

Wifebeater Bob

THE BENNINGTON PLAZA HOTEL/Apartments is located on Wilshire Boulevard in West L.A., not far from where Orange Juice Simpson sliced off the head of his sexy blonde wife, then watched her blood run down the sidewalk into a landscaped bed of begonias.

The building is tall. Upscale. The hotel room and condominium prices at the Bennington range from high to very high. I became familiar with the place because I had a "steady" staying there—a stockbroker guy named Amir from New York. Amir was raised in Manhattan and never learned to drive, so when he temporarily relocated to L.A., he used taxis for all his transportation. It was my cab that was head-out in the feed line at LAX the day Amir walked through the ARRIVALS doors at American Airlines.

I had been back working a cabbie gig as a result of my need for money. And insanity. After our last blowup, a pissy misunderstanding about me selling her signed copy of *Grapes of Wrath*, my girlfriend Debra moved out, then mailed me a ransom note from the P.O. box of a friend. She refused all communication and was holding my manuscript until I paid back the value of the book. Her way of getting even. I'd been working on my new novel daily for eighteen months. Her demand was for me to send $600 a month until the five grand was paid in full. If I missed one extortion installment, she would burn my pages and I would never see the manuscript again. Me and Debra had had a good run together, until she gave up vodka and found Jesus.

Hack driver is the only occupation I know about with no boss, and because I have always performed poorly at supervised employment, I returned to the taxi business. The upside, now that I was working again, was that my own boozing was under control and I was on beer only, except for my days off.

AMIR FROM NEW YORK and I had a deal. A six-month contract. Every morning I would pick him up at the main entrance to the Bennington at 6:35, hit the 405, then the 10 Freeway East, then the 110 North, and have him downtown on Spring Street at his brokerage house job by seven o'clock. In the afternoon, at 5:00, the process was reversed. On weekends I drove him and his friends to the Beverly Hills shops or to the movies or the bars on Santa Monica Boulevard in West Hollywood. Amir was gay and not especially talkative, even after we got to know each other, but he was one helluva good tipper.

Because I was around the Bennington Plaza so often in my taxi, I got to know the hotel's doorman on a one-to-one basis. His name was Bob. Bob was older than me, in his fifties and, at first sight, regal looking in his British footman's get-up with top hat and epaulets. And Bob was tall. At least six-foot-five. He might easily have been mistaken for a TV actor with his square jaw, slow speech, and snazzy western boots, but the more a person cultivated a speaking relationship with Bob, the more he came to regret it. Bob's basic problem as a doorman and a human was that he was a fuck. He lacked decency and a stable personality.

On my off time from driving Amir, I began hanging out with a few of the cabbies who worked the hack line at the side of the Bennington. In L.A. the taxi industry is an amalgam of misfits and gypsies: musician-wannabes, unemployed screen writers, Vietnam vets, ex-dopers, and Middle East immigrants. One of these guys was Sid Cohen, an owner-driver. Sid was a bright guy with a malevolent sense of humor. Once he'd been an advance man and organizer for political campaigns, and for a few years he'd even written a column for a newspaper in Michigan. Me and Sid had coffee together frequently and shot the shit. He and his twenty-year-old Benz taxi were fixtures at the Bennington, and Sid knew the dirt on everybody who worked at the hotel. Especially doorman Bob.

Sid enthusiastically despised Bob and had coined a name for him: "Wifebeater Bob." This handle was Sid's idea of an "in" joke. Bob wasn't actually a spousal abuser. In fact, it was his red-haired wife, Patsy, who supposedly was the violent one.

The two of them had arrived at the Bennington Plaza at the same time six months before. Patsy ran the maid and maintenance service while slow-thinking Bob took over for the retiring doorman. The Wifebeater Bob gag got started as follows: one morning in their first week on the job, according to Sid, Patsy discovered her husband on duty with gin on his breath and discarded her sanity. She began attacking the big goof in the hotel's parking lot. Tall Bob was taken down a peg.

But after that, shit began rolling downhill. Wifebeater Bob underwent a spontaneous personality rearrangement. For the worse. To even the score for his public humiliation and lousy marriage, he upped his alcohol intake and launched a daily terrorism campaign on all those unlucky enough to fall under his authority at the hotel. This included four bellmen, a half dozen Latino parking lot guys, and the subcategory of taxi drivers. Doorman Bob had morphed himself into a giant pain in the ass.

Because the jerk was now a consistent morning boozer, with coffee, by the time the midafternoon slowdown rolled around he would easily have gone through his first of two daily pints of gin and be jonesing for a drink. It was especially at these times that Bob reached the nadir of his most evil vengefulness.

On his lunch break, on his way to the liquor store or to his van for pint number two, the belligerent asshole in the Buckingham Palace uniform made it a habit to stroll down the taxi line, top hat cocked over his eyes, and confront various drivers. I'd seen this for myself.

Bob's favorite target was Sid Cohen. Sid was sure he'd been singled out because, from the first, he'd refused to pay Wifebeater Bob any kickbacks. And add to that that the doorman correctly suspected it was Sid who was the one responsible for the nickname. (The handle had lately made its way inside the hotel, to the pleasure and amusement of the rest of the staff.)

When Wifebeater Bob saw Sid's taxi on the hack line his aggression could be scary. One particular day, after I returned from dropping Amir downtown, I was a witness to him going completely nuts.

"Yo, asshole," Bob snarled, leaning his pink head inside Sid's driver's window, pointing a chrome whistle in his face. "You think I'm a chump, right? Some kyna bitch. Last week you got a fifty-dollar fuckin' round-trip airport rip to LAX from my hotel, on my shift, and whaddid I get back from you? I got zip. No bird dog. Nuthin'. How 'bout this, Sid, you cheap rat bastard. How 'bout next time you make it up to the head after two hours in my cab line, I give you a chickenshit three-dollar-and-twenty-cent fare to Westwood? I bet you won't think that's funny, will ya, you tight-assed prick." Then Bob commenced to pound on the roof of Sid's Benz.

Drunk or sober, Wifebeater Bob made it a habit to go out of his way to get even with those he felt had crossed him.

The real problem for Sid and the other guys who worked the taxi line was that there are few good, high-volume hotels on the west side of Los Angeles, and the Bennington is probably the best of the bunch. Sid and the other cabbies had been there long before Wifebeater Bob arrived and had no intention of moving on or submitting to greasing the schizophrenic doorman. It was a bad situation and it was getting worse by the day.

But things had been going better than okay for me. From the beginning of driving Amir, I had paid my monthly extortion payments to my ex-girlfriend on time, and me and the doorman had not seriously bumped heads. This was because I had little occasion to work the hack line. I'd avoided the verbal muggings and demands for kickbacks.

But one morning that all changed. Bob had the second of his public run-ins with Patsy. This time it was at the service entrance to the hotel. Patsy caught her old man taking a snort from the short dog in his hip pocket, pitched a nutfit, and began pummeling him with kicks to the legs and hooks to the head.

I was in the hotel's employee bathroom taking a squirt, and when I came out the side door, I witnessed the action first-hand. In the wind-up, Patsy smashed her husband's gin bottle against the basement's concrete steps, bloodied his lip, then confiscated his wallet.

When it was over, not wanting to get involved or allow my mouth to make a comment that might cause trouble for me later, I slipped across the alley to my cab, got in, and took off.

That's when my trouble started. Ten minutes later I was a block away at a liquor store on Wilshire, making a malt liquor purchase, when emasculated Bob walked up behind me at the register. He had entered the place just after I did. His lip was still bleeding, and he had insufficient funds in his pocket to pay for a half pint.

Shaking badly and in need of his bracer, Bob recognized me. "Yo, Shorty," he whispered, pulling me down the long counter in front of the magazine rack, "you seen me back there at the hotel with Patsy. Just now. Right?"

I tried hedging. "My cab was parked by the side of the building," I said.

"Thaz right. I seen you. You was fuckin' there. Don't bullshit me. So, what about it?"

"What about what?"

"You gonna keep your mouth shut?"

I began walking away. "Your personal issues are not my concern," I said.

Now the jerk was in my face and had me by the sleeve of my jacket. "I'm sayin', will you keep quiet about what you just seen? I mean to the others. I don't want no gossip getting back to the manager. Yes or no, Shorty?"

I pushed his arm off. "Do not touch me," I snarled.

"I know you're friends with that cocksucker Sid. I'm warnin' ya, Shorty, don't mess with me. Ya hear?"

"In point of fact, my name is Bruno. I dislike being referred to as Shorty."

"Huh? What's wrong with—Shorty?"

"Let's just say I'm sensitive about my height. Think of me as the only one of the seven dwarfs that Snow White refused to fuck."

"Whaz that supposta mean?"

"Forget it moron."

"I knew you was messin' with me."

"No, I'm not," I said. "For the last time, your absurd domestic issues hold no interest for me."

Wifebeater Bob looked me up and down in an attempt to convince himself I wasn't a rat. Then he smiled. "Okay, fair enough," he whispered. "Then gimme a buck. I need a dollar more to get me my short dog."

I'd been rattled by the exchange. I dug in my pocket and handed him the money.

Bob paid for his bottle and was still in the store after I left.

I crossed the sidewalk and was about to get into my cab when he was behind me again, restraining me by the sleeve of my jacket. This time I was ushered around the side of the building to the parking lot. There, out of view of the street traffic, I pried his hand away.

He was leering and out of breath. Unscrewing the cap

from his half pint, the red-nosed imbecile wiped drying blood from his lip and took a long slam. "Listen, my man," he whispered, after lowering his jug and exhaling deeply, "I owe you."

I hated this absurd doofus. My sole desire was to escape from his sweaty Neanderthal hands, his bad temper and bad breath. But he was the Bennington's doorman and I told myself it was unwise to cross him. "Forget it," I said back. "I don't care. Pay me or don't pay me."

Bob took another long slam that emptied his jug. "I ain't talkin' about the money. You'll see, Shorty. Just you remember what I said and keep your fucking trap shut."

"I need to get back to work."

The goon was smiling. "You wait. Juss wait. Old Bob never forgets a favor. You can bet your mother's stinky skivvies on it."

"My mother is deceased, asshole."

WITH THAT I CROSSED the parking lot to where my cab was parked at the curb, got in, locked the doors, and started the engine.

Sitting behind the wheel, I felt as though my hair was on fire. I looked back. Wifebeater Bob was still standing against the wall, smoking a cigarette. I despised being grabbed and bullied. But now that I was alone, there was something else that was making me far more uncomfortable: self-disgust. What was wrong with me? Why had I not said what was in my gut? I could have used the fight with his wife against him, confronted the prick at his level, then intimidated him into mending his behavior. Instead I'd let the opportunity pass. The fear of jeopardizing my income and sweet deal with Amir had made me hesitate. For months I'd thought of nothing but getting my manuscript back. Now my obsession had rendered me a coward. A cheesedick. This tyrant fuck had ruined the hotel for a dozen cabbies. Men who busted their asses six and seven days a week trying to make a living. I'd had my chance to do something, but my only concern was covering my ass.

THAT NIGHT, AFTER WORK, after I arrived home, my brain refused to let go of the incident. Sitting in my darkened apartment, I smoked cigarettes and drank warm beer continuing to replay my weakness. Shame and self-mocking congested my thoughts like the stink of alley piss.

To clear my mind, I decided I would write a letter to my ex-girlfriend. Since the theft of the manuscript, I'd been immobilized by her treachery. My creativity had gone to shit. I was dried up. A dead man. There had been two previous notes from me, both spiteful and ill-advised, enclosed with other payments. They had gone unanswered. Only the canceled checks came back in the mail.

Going to my desk, I turned on the overhead lamp, clicked on my electric typewriter, and cranked in a piece of paper. This time would be different. I would compose a letter of resolution, somehow find the words to free myself from the teetotaling vampire Jesus twat who had destroyed my character and ruined my life. I would say that our troubles were entirely my fault. It didn't matter. Nothing mattered. Whatever the cost, I had to have my book back.

But twenty minutes later, the page in my typewriter was still blank. I couldn't do it. My brain and my fingers had failed me. I gave up in a rage. Insane. Ripping the paper out of the carriage, I threw it across the room, then smashed my half-full beer can against the wall.

In my refrigerator/freezer there was most of a fifth of Stoli. I poured four fingers into a dirty glass, then turned the light off. By midnight the vodka was gone and I was drunk.

I began dialing phone sex numbers from the out-call massage section of the *L.A. Weekly*, then spent an hour chatting with a girl who called herself Erin-Lee. Erin-Lee said they'd piped my call in to her at home, and she was in her bedroom wearing no bra and red thong panties. She said she liked my voice and that us speaking anonymously like this made her pussy wet. She wanted to know if me talking to her turned me on too. Was my cock hard? I said it was. She insisted that I write down her private answer phone number—just in case— and let me know that she charged a hundred bucks for an in-person blowjob. I could call her any time.

Following that, I was made to listen to a preposterous tale involving her Ford Escort. According to Erin-Lee, the car had blown its transmission. She wanted me to stay on the line for another half an hour. If I did, it would be a gigantic-amazing favor and totally-fuckin'-fabulous of me because she would then have the last sixty bucks she needed to pay her mechanic for his work. Erin-Lee whispered that she wanted us both to cum at the same time.

"Sure," I said. "No problem. I've got nothing else to do. My flight to Athens isn't leaving until tomorrow night."

TWO MORNINGS LATER AFTER my day off, when I arrived at the Bennington for my usual pickup, Amir surprised me by checking out one month early. Instead of taking him downtown to his brokerage house, I drove my New York client and his six suitcases to the airport for the last time. He was going home to Riverside Drive.

Getting out at the United terminal, he shook my hand but avoided eye contact. For five months this guy had exhibited the charm and personal warmth of a Korea town produce vendor. Now, from his inside coat pocket, Amir handed me an envelope containing ten one-hundred-dollar bills. He was smiling. "Consider this as two weeks' severance pay," he said.

Leaving the airport, I stopped at the post office on Century Boulevard. Inside, I located a big cardboard Priority Mail envelope and stuffed the money inside. While I waited in line, I scribbled a note in longhand: "Debra, you know I love you! Goddammit, I'm sorry. Please come home."

I HAD NOT YET had the opportunity to discuss Wifebeater Bob's latest public disgrace with Sid and the other guys, but now I was resolved to do just that. With Amir gone, as it stood, I had nothing to protect at the Bennington and nothing to lose.

On my way back to the hotel I came up with a plan and invented a new, better-fitting account of my run-in at the liquor store with the doorman. I'd tell the guys at the hack line how I had been an eyewitness to Wifebeater Bob's newest ass-kicking and, in the aftermath, seized my chance to settle accounts for us all. I'd let them know the way I'd gotten right into the jerk's greedy, bloated face. How I'd tweaked and lost my cool, then gone chest-to-chest with the huge psycho, instructing him, in no uncertain terms, to either back off with his cab driver threats and bribe money demands or face me and the ugly consequences. To underscore this exaggerated version of the facts, I'd decided to include the part where I'd stabbed my finger directly against the end of his nose. "Go ahead," I'd snarled, "try fucking with me! Call my bluff! I'll go right to the hotel manager. By next week you and that crazy bitch wife of yours will be pushing shopping carts up Wilshire Boulevard."

BACK AT THE BENNINGTON, I wheeled my cab to the rear of the hack line and got out. Sid waved hello. He and Vietnam Cuz were leaning against one of the cabs, smoking and talking.

My determination was at its peak and I was ready to shift into action.

I locked my taxi's door and jammed the key deep in my pants pocket. All that was left now was for me to face Wifebeater Bob in private for five minutes with my demands, but first I'd tip off the guys that something big was about to happen.

Just then the doorman's whistle blew—the signal for everyone in line to move up—and the first cab to come forward and take the next fare.

We all returned to our cars and were about to reposition

ourselves when Bob's whistle blew again. Twenty-five yards away, he was holding up his hand in a "stop" gesture.

The whistle blew a third time. Bob was pointing at me and my cab, waving me along to come ahead.

Swinging my rattling Chevy out past the other cars, I pulled around the hotel drive, then stopped at the main entrance.

The big doorman came around to my driver's window and leaned in. He looked pleased with himself. But before he could open his mouth, I cut loose. "Okay, asshole," I barked. "You and I need to talk. Now!"

"Save it, Shorty," Bob whispered.

"Right now, I said!"

"Hey look, I got two pieces coming out. A mother and daughter from Austin. First time in town. They're going to Disneyland."

"Forget it. I'm not interested. That's final."

"Oh, okay. How about if it's an all-day fare? Wait and return. I told the lady it would cost her a flat two-fifty."

"Two-fifty? You told her two hundred and fifty to Disney-land and back?"

"Sure. There's waiting time, right?"

"I don't believe you."

"No? Well, they're on their way down in the elevator right now . . . So, whatcha wanna do, hotshot, bust my chops or make some money?"

My tongue was stuck.

Wifebeater Bob was sneering. "This ain't no game show, Ace. It's cash money. Yes or no? In or out?

"Okay," was the word that came out from between my lips. "Okay, I'll take it."

He had me.

ON MY WAY TO Disneyland with Mrs. Dwan and her daughter, Mimi, my stomach was knotted. Two hundred and fifty bucks was two days' pay. Only a fool would have said no. Bob had played me perfectly.

When I returned to the hotel that night to drop off Mrs. Dwan and Mimi, the doorman had gone home and the hack line was empty of cabs. Mrs. Dwan handed me three one-hundred-dollar bills, smiled, then told me to keep the change.

THE NEXT MORNING, AT just after seven o'clock, I swung my cab into the Bennington's taxi holding line. Again, it was empty. Morning rush hour was keeping all the cabbies busy. There was Wifebeater Bob positioned under the hotel awning. When he saw my cab, he whistled excitedly for me to come forward.

Pulling around the circular drive, I stopped with my back door even with the walkway carpeting.

Bob took his time strolling around to my driver's window. Eighteen inches away, I could smell the gin on his breath. "So howdit go yesterday?" he slurred, patting my arm. "Missus Dwan and her kid?"

"Why?"

"Din Old Bob tell you he never forgets a favor?"

I pushed his hand off. "Blow me, Old Bob."

The remark appeared to have no effect. "Din I tell you I'd take care of you? So how much did you collect, bottom line?"

"My income is none of your concern."

Wifebeater Bob's arms were folded across his chest. "Wrong answer, pal. We're partners. One hand washes the other. I want my cut from yesterday."

"What cut?"

"Thirty percent. Fair is fair."

"I think not, Old Bob. Go fuck yourself."

"It's that or you go to the back of the hack line with your pal Sid. Old Bob don't mind givin' his goodies to the other guys."

"Hear this, dickless! I was there the other day. At the side entrance. I watched you—moron Wifebeater Bob—get your ass kicked by a five-foot-tall redhead. I saw it all. Remember? So, fuck you! It's my turn now. I'm going inside to have a little talk with the hotel manager."

What happened next happened quickly. I was pulled from my taxi and there were a series of punches. In the end I found myself on the pavement bleeding from my nose. It took three parking lot guys to pull the drunken goof off me.

TWO WEEKS LATER EVERYTHING at the Bennington was back to normal. My taxi had been permanently barred from the premises, and I had taken a limo gig courtesy of a friend of Sid Cohen. Sid's pal owned his own private car service. Because the doorman's wife had a cousin and that cousin was the chain's GM, no action whatever was taken against Wifebeater Bob.

The half-juiced asshole was on his morning break, in his van at the corner of the parking lot, when one of the cabbies from the line approached the vehicle with Bob's wife close behind. As me and half a dozen of the guys watched from a distance, Patsy unlocked the van's sliding door with her key and pulled it open. Inside, Wifebeater Bob was being orally serviced by a hooker named Erin-Lee. It was the best hundred bucks I'd ever spent.

I had come to a decision regarding my relationships with women: next time I got drunk and sold a girlfriend's signed first edition of *Grapes of Wrath,* I'd come clean instead of acting surprised, then insisting we'd been burglarized. Of secondary consideration was my opinion that John Steinbeck was wordy and, at best, a mediocre literary talent.

Mae West

THESE WERE STRANGE DAYS. Everything I touched seemed to be turning to pain. Even Kerri's dog Banana hated me.

In the beginning, the month I first moved in, I'd made up this game: I would hold up two fingers to the animal in a sort of "V" for victory, Nixon-type signal, then whisper his name. "Ba-Nana." "Ba-Nana."

It pissed the dog off. I knew it pissed him off, but I did it anyway. Mostly it was when I was on the juice that I did it but in retrospect I can see that I'm responsible for instigating our mutual hatred. I don't like dogs. The pig is my animal of preference. And I was unable to bond with Kerri's little rat-faced fucker so, for fun, I tormented him almost every time the opportunity arose.

After a while it became automatic, and I enjoyed it. Kerri would be out of the room getting a beer or in the john, or paying for the pizza at the front door, and me and the dog would be alone for a few seconds. I'd just hold up the fingers and whisper "Ba-Nana," to the little shit, and he would go crazy and start snarling.

My girlfriend's courtyard apartment was just off La Brea Avenue on Hollywood Boulevard. A nice one-bedroom with a patio and an unused garden area for her mutt. The rooms had lots of light and space. Perfect for a writer.

But unhappily, over time, my arrangement with Banana's master was deteriorating. I didn't completely understand why, but I knew that she disliked my boozing and my contentious point of view while intoxicated.

In short order, I had gone from Kerri's bar mate, to roommate, to dead weight. But she wouldn't face me with the information. Unlike other women I had lived with, Kerri lacked the chops for blunt confrontation. I was reasonably sure that she had come to view our relationship as a mistake.

The living arrangement was okay for me, and I was content for the most part, but my roomie held grudges. A silent disapproval campaign was under way.

It began by her coming to sleep in a T-shirt. Our bedtime fun had always been good, and after an evening of booze she was a class-A slut and game for any of my unusual sexual requests, but that stopped. Abruptly. Soon after, to underscore her discontent, she even quit drinking.

Eventually, as these moves failed to produce the desired effect, she upped the ante. The apartment's supply of liquor dried up, and I was left daily with unwashed dishes and the garbage to take out. At night, when she returned from her job, my attempts at conversation were greeted by a series of negative one-liners followed by quiet scorn. Any fool would conclude that Kerri was displeased. Naturally, so was fucking Banana. But in my observation, tactics like these work better on pets than on humans.

Coincidentally, the time we stopped screwing overlapped with the time the dog actually began attempts to attack me. At first the coward would only snarl when Kerri was present in the room to defend him. All other times, especially when she was at work, he knew to keep his distance. The fuzzy shit-runt spent the bulk of his day in the bedroom protecting her side of the bed. If he stayed out of my way, I was usually content to leave him alone. It was primarily in the evening, after I'd had a couple of drinks, that me and the dog conflicted. Kerri would be distracted switching the TV or talking on the phone. I'd catch Banana's eye and commence my two-finger salute. He'd growl, then feign a charge. The animal's conduct was getting more and more menacing.

For me, three days a week driving a taxi had not been cutting it. My writing was going well and two of my poems had been accepted by a classy English quarterly from Wrecking Ball Press. But poetry magazines pay a writer almost nothing, and I was barely able to support myself from the taxi money, so household contributions fell into the category of an extravagance I could ill afford.

Kerri knew that I fancied myself a writer and that I spent a good part of my time reading or at the typewriter. She'd been well aware of my financial status when we made the deal for me to become her live-in, but now this issue was becoming another bone of contention.

Things came to a head late one Friday night in the middle of a Scrabble game. I had had my share of frozen vodka from the fridge and I was not myself, eighty-three points down, and in an evil mood. While Kerri was visiting the fridge, I whispered "Banana" and made my customary "V" sign. The odious little prick had stationed himself for the evening on the floor beneath her chair.

Suddenly, I was set upon by the snarling bastard. He sank his fangs into my khakis, scraped my ankle, and tore through one cuff. In self-defense, I swatted him away with my chair cushion. Two or three times.

Kerri did not see her animal assault me. All she could have witnessed was me flailing the chair pad as she rushed in from the kitchen. When Banana charged again, I began pushing him off with my foot.

"You're kicking my dog!" she screamed. "You'll kill him! Stop it!"

"I am not! Don't be stupid! He bit me."

"Stupid? You prickshit! You're calling me STUPID!? You're the fucking cab driver!"

"Christ almighty, can't you see that your dog's attacking me?"

"Get out, you son-of-a-bitch! Get out of my house!"

"Be reasonable. Call the animal off!"

But the damage was done. Five minutes later she was locked in the bedroom with Banana, threatening a call to 9-1-1 and the spousal abuse hot line.

KERRI HELD THE JOB of day manager at Ameche's, a pasta and steak house in Marina del Rey. It was there that we'd met a year before, at the bar, and it was also there that she told her problems to one of her coworkers, a fussy, big-titted twat hostess named Sonja.

After spilling her guts about the dog attack and my animosity toward Banana and describing our deteriorating domestic situation, Sonja had made the diagnosis that her friend's only solution was to curb my drinking. To her, I sounded like a basically decent schmuck, except for the booze. According to what Kerri said later, in Sonja's view, writers are self-indulgent and lazy. There wasn't much hope for cultivation there, but in her own life she had been able to get her husband off the sauce by way of a drug called Antabuse. Threats of divorce and the use of the medication had enabled him to see the light. Three months later their relationship was back on track.

MAKE NO MISTAKE, ANTABUSE is evil shit. If you drink alcohol within twenty-four hours after injecting this crap for a few days, your heart rate will double, you will turn bright red, and soon you will be puking up your guts. It's tough retribution, but it was the ultimatum facing me when my long-legged roommate arrived home from work that evening.

I was handed a blue-and-white pamphlet about alcohol and drug therapy. On it was stamped the name of a clinic in Hollywood where Antabuse is dispensed free of charge.

Imagine being on a government appropriations committee allocating the funds to research a joyless rat-snot compound like Antabuse. Or being a senator approving the eighty-million-dollar (or whatever) budget for the production of a medication that will inflict sickness on someone having a glass of wine with dinner. Men in a room agreeing to stomp out the godless ingestion of the wine cooler. Think about the conversations these bloodsucking, rectumless bureaucrats must've had. The delight they shared in knowing they would be poisoning some poor schlump sitting by his TV on Sunday afternoon, drinking a can of beer while watching his ball game. Maybe the same ghoul cocksucker who invented methadone is the same genius they called in to come up with Antabuse. And everyone knows what a great success methadone became. What a boon to social justice that toxic venom turned out to be.

Along with the literature Kerri slapped into my hand came the threat of the ax. I was a rummy. A bad-tempered loser. I had one of two choices: sign up or pack up. And leave the fucking dog alone. She'd had enough.

THE EAST HOLLYWOOD ALCOHOL and Drug Relief Program was located on Melrose Avenue. Two days later I found myself in their waiting room, a clipboard on my lap, filling out a registration questionnaire.

The lady, my area's coordinator, was named Ms. Consuela. When I was ushered in, she made firm eye contact, then told me to have a seat.

She looked over my answers, made a face, then folded her hands on the desk. "So, consumption-wise, do you drink every day?"

"I don't keep track," I said. "Basically, I suppose, one or two beers a day. Sometimes a mixed drink. That's usually about it."

My reply was inadequate for Consuela. "Be specific, please. Let's not waste each other's time here."

"Okay, I drink every day. How's that?

"One or two beers or a cocktail? That's all you drink?"

"No. Usually more, I guess."

"The truth, please. We require complete candor. It will facilitate your recovery."

I paused here to consider her question and be accurate, but Consuela was making her face again. "Hey," I said. "Give me a second, okay? Can I have a goddamn second?"

She checked a box on her form and went on. "When do you feel your alcohol consumption became out of control? How long has it been since the onset of your abnormal drinking?"

"Okay ... wait ... my alcohol consumption is not out of control. My girlfriend is the one who has decided I drink too much."

Ms. Consuela was a short woman with a pissy, intolerant, head-nurse, chickenshit disposition. "We're done," she announced. She stood up.

"So, will you be prescribing Antabuse for me?"

"Absolutely not. I said we're done."

"How come I don't get the Antabuse?"

"You don't need it. Have a nice day, sir."

Now I was on my feet too. "Look," I said, "that's the reason I'm here. Jesus, that's why I sat in your waiting room for forty minutes filling out the goddamn questionnaire. I checked the place that asked if I wanted alcohol treatment. Look at the form. You're committing an oversight."

"Sir, you just told me to my face that your alcohol consumption is not out of control. Ten seconds ago you said you do NOT have a drinking problem."

Time to backpedal. "Okay, I lied. I understated my condition. I DO have a drinking problem. Okay?"

Consuela's arms were folded across her chest. "Which is it, sir? If you're here to take the heat off or to get a spouse or girlfriend off your back, then you've come to the wrong clinic. Antabuse therapy is not a quick fix. And we don't do couples counseling."

"Okay. Okay. I'm here for me. I need the drugs. I can't stop drinking. Is that what you need to hear?"

Ms. Consuela sat down. "Better," she whiffed. "In our experience, denial is the hallmark symptom of alcoholism."

I sat again but began fidgeting with my car keys.

"Stop that," Consuela said. "Put those keys in your pocket, sir."

"Jesus, what is this, the fucking Inquisition?"

"Distractions annoy me. I am attempting to qualify you for drug and alcohol treatment. The process requires your complete attention. Is that plainly clear?"

"I know a dog I'd like to introduce to you. His name is Banana."

"Is that some sort of threat, sir? What is the precise meaning of that remark?"

I slid my car keys into my pocket. "Okay. Can we go on?"

"And knock off the profanity."

"I apologize."

Ms. Consuela wrote my name at the top of an intake form. "I am now going to ask you a series of questions. Answer truthfully and there's a good possibility that you'll be selected for our outpatient services. Understood?"

"Understood. Great. I'm ready."

"Have you ever been arrested as a result of intoxication?"

"Yes."

"How many times?"

"Several times . . . Well, okay, what I mean is, are you including drunk-driving tickets too?"

"Everything. Public intoxication. Intoxication in a motor vehicle. Spousal abuse while under the influence. All of it. How many times?"

(As a cab driver, to protect my ability to earn a living, for many years I had been in possession of two drivers licenses, one from New York with a slightly different last name and one from California in my real name. The two times I got popped for drunk driving in L.A. were when I was in my own car and I gave the cop my New York license. Of course, there was no way I would divulge this shit to Consuela or discuss the other license.) "Three times, I think," I said.

"You think?"

"Five times total. I'm sure it's five. I was just trying to think back."

Consuela made a check mark on her form. "Next question: Have you ever been hospitalized for alcohol abuse?"

"I've been in detox once. No. Wait. Twice. Make it two."

Ms. Consuela checked another box, then picked up a black marker and drew a big "X" through the rest of the form. She turned the paper around and pushed it across the table, then handed me a pen. "Sign on the bottom," she demanded.

"What am I signing?"

"You qualify for therapy and Antabuse treatment. You are signing my intake form that permits you to receive medication and out-patient services."

I signed the paper then pushed it back. "What kind of out-patient services?"

"Twice a week at 7:00 a.m. you will be required to be here to take your medication in the presence of a facilitator and then have counseling sessions."

"Look, I work too. How long does this stuff take?"

"The entire process lasts about ninety minutes."

"Okay, but suppose I'm sick or something and can't come that day?"

"You will be disqualified after your second no-show in any calendar month. You start now. Today. See Dr. Fogel in the office next door."

"Today? There's no grace period?"

Consuela was on her feet again. "Sir, your grace period was all the years you drove a taxi on the streets of this city drunk and didn't kill a child. You've had your grace period. See Dr. Fogel next door."

THAT DAY, AFTER MORE waiting, I saw Dr. Fogel for five minutes, then took my first pill and signed another form. That was Tuesday.

On Thursday I saw Fogel again for five minutes, said I felt

fine, signed his paper, then stood in line with the other guys to take my pill. The rest of the days between appearances everyone was unmonitored and on the honor system. But I made a commitment to myself to stick with the deal, and I didn't drink or try to drink.

At home the arrangement was on the way to restoration. A couple of nights later Kerri came to bed without her T-shirt as an incentive and complimented me for valuing our relationship. When I asked her if she would mind putting her animal in the living room and closing the bedroom door, so I could lick her pussy and asshole in peace, she didn't hesitate at all.

I reported to work for the next three days in a row and made an average of $150 a day in my cab. The following morning, on my day off, after a cum-swallowing blowjob, I decided to give my roommate a hundred bucks for household expenses.

IN MY EXPERIENCE, EVERYTHING in life has its angles and loopholes. By the end of my first full week, I discovered that the Antabuse drug program could be "worked" to the client's personal satisfaction.

It was on the following Tuesday that I was waiting outside the clinic, smoking and queued up to see Dr. Fogel, who had fallen behind in his five-minute counseling sessions. The guy standing by the front door's concrete ashtray with me was named Bernie. I'd seen him twice. We both "dosed" on the same schedule.

Bernie struck me as an affable cat, quiet-spoken and pleasant. I liked his hat too, a black short-brimmed number that was common to many of the blues players in the '60s and '70s. Next to him on the asphalt was his horn, a saxophone, in its case. Bernie was a film studio musician. Unlike me, he was court ordered and on five years' probation for his third drunk-driving charge.

Standing there talking and smoking, our conversation became confidential. He leaned in and asked me how long it'd been since I had a taste.

"My last drink was exactly seven days ago, the day I started on the program," I said.

"Uuuuuhhhhh, brother, that's a long dry patch. How you keepin'?"

"Shit, I'm thirsty. I lose my temper at everybody. I'm about to kill my girlfriend's dog. Truth is, I'm pretty shaky."

"B" was grinning. He twisted his body to the side and flashed the cap of a short dog stashed in the pocket of his leather jacket. Then he looked around to check the parking lot for spies. When the coast was clear, he unscrewed the cap and took a long hit.

"Man, you crazy?" I said.

He passed me the jug. "I usually only drink shit where the label moves. You know, like Night Train, and Thunderbird. And Ripple. This's Triple Jack. Mean shit. I had to settle. Gahead, hit it. Hit it good," he said. "Hey, we deserve it, right?"

"No way."

"Man, fuck them pills. Don't you know the gag about them pills?"

"Tell me, for chrissake. I'm standing here in the desert. Jonesing. I've been half nuts all week."

"Simple shit, my man. If you hit the stuff within the first hour after you drop your pill, you can skate until the next time you come in. When you leave here, throw out the rest of the meds they gave you."

"What happens then? What about the piss test?"

"Bring in your own piss, man. Don't be a chump. They let you go into the bathroom by yourself with the test vial, right?"

"Yeah."

"Well . . ."

"What about the meds? Didn't you get sick?"

"Okay, you could get a little spell at first. I won't lie. You might even puke the first or second time out, but after that you're clear. Peace returns. The trick is to drink in the first half hour after you drop the pill. The alcohol counteracts the pill. But only take the two pills a week. Take the shit only when you have to, when you're being supervised."

"How sick do you get?"

"You see me sippin' at my dog here. Bro, like I say, trick is to hit your jug right away. Now. Don't go doin' it later on or you WILL be sicker'n shit. I know. I mean, MAN, I KNOW. Hit it now. Go for it while nobody's looking."

I took the bag from Bernie's hand, held it up to my mouth, and hit it good. A long slam. My relief was instant.

THE DAY AFTER KERRI again ordered me out of the apartment, Banana bit me on the thigh. I'd returned to her place for my stuff, my last boxes and clothes and additional belongings. Without provocation, the fucker lunged at me.

Later that evening, when I came back for my typewriter case, she was sitting on her couch, a fifth of bourbon in front of her, half drunk and crying. The dog was gone, she sobbed. Disappeared. He had run off.

At her instruction, that same day, Bob the manager came by to change the locks. Later on, in tears, when she knocked at his apartment, the guy conceded that he might have left the front door open while he was doing his work. Bottom line, ratdog was now on his own.

Me and Kerri had a drink together and I attempted to console her, saying stuff like "You'll see, he'll turn up."

"I thought you hated him," she sniffed. "You kicked him."

"C'mon, that was an error committed in the heat of the moment. Anyway, hate isn't the right word. Sure, he bit me and all but, bottom line, we just never hit it off. In fact," I added, "I blame myself."

"I tried calling you three times today. You were at work, weren't you? Didn't you get my messages?"

"Yeah," I said, the lie coming out effortlessly, "I picked the messages up when I turned in. I hadn't had any sleep, so I took a town car out this morning on the day line. I wound up doing airport runs all day."

I brought a bag of ice in from the kitchen and we talked things through. One subject led to another and finally our differences were ironed out. The windup was that I spent the night and moved my stuff back in from the trunk of my car.

THE NEXT DAY AT Kinko's Copies on Hollywood Boulevard, carrying out my promise to my girlfriend, I xeroxed fifty flyers featuring Banana's photograph and tacked and taped them up everywhere within a ten-block radius of the apartment.

Kerri went to work but kept leaving messages on the apartment's answering machine, demanding updates.

No Banana. No trace.

A couple of weeks later she seemed to be coming to terms with her loss, but to my disappointment, our relationship and the living situation were back in the shithouse. During a dinner event with Sonja from work and her henpecked husband, sober Leo, at our apartment, after a bit too much wine I made an inappropriate remark and the couple left early. The next day the ultimatum was the same as before: get help for the boozing or move out.

THE METROPOLITAN CENTER FOR Hypnotherapy is on Sunset Boulevard two blocks west of La Brea. Kerri saw the sign on her way home from her restaurant job and wrote down the address and phone number:

CURE SMOKING, SEXUAL DYSFUNCTION, OVEREATING, ALCOHOL AND DRUG PROBLEMS. RESULTS GUARANTEED.

I went for the free consultation and had a one-hour meeting with Orlin Edward O'Hagan, PhD. Old O'Hagan was cofounder of the place. He showed me pages and pages of testimonial letters from clients who had lost weight, quit heroin, and could now get their dick hard. In the end, I signed up for the sixty-day plan and began treatment.

The upside to hypnotherapy is that it is effortless. The downside is that it isn't cheap. But Kerri is a generous girl.

Once the client and the doctor have come to terms regarding the results they want to achieve, the rest is easy. A series of ninety-minute recorded tapes are made.

Three nights a week at 8:00 I walked the four blocks from Kerri's apartment to the office on Sunset. Once there and on time, I was escorted into a small room with headphones, a blackout mask, and a reclining chair. When all the gear was in place and I was lying back, someone clicked on a switch and the piped-in recording began. The only words I ever recall hearing on the tape came in O'Hagan's melodious voice. "You are deeply relaxed ... deeply, deeply relaxed. A feeling of peace and ease now fills every fiber of your being ..." Ninety minutes later I got up and walked home.

The significant part of the hypnotherapy treatment, for me, was that it actually began to work right away. My shakes left almost immediately and within days I had tapered down to one or two beers. Budweiser began to have a bitter, rancid taste and even hard liquor took on the flavor of ashes. After that, every time I tried a drink I was turned off. A couple of weeks later I realized that I had no desire left for the stuff and from that day on I was sober.

The only negative side effect was that I had lost my desire to write. I could sit for an hour with a blank sheet of paper in my typewriter and not put down a full sentence. The things that had always driven me, my rage and my impatience and my disgust for America's TV culture and the film business and lousy, pulp-selling fraud writers no longer seemed to fire me up.

Orlin O'Hagan told me not to worry. He said all artists had their up and down periods. I was going through an adjustment phase. It was all pretty normal. But I was unhappy and felt my life had lost its sense of purpose.

KERRI AND I WERE BACK on solid footing again, and as a gesture of support she made sure to steer clear of ordering wine or beer when we went out to eat. She even began to discuss a trip to the L.A. pound and the possibility of adopting a new dog. I quickly discouraged the idea by telling her that Banana still might turn up.

ONE EVENING I RECEIVED a call from Bernie, the film musician I'd met at the Antabuse program. He lived not far from our neighborhood and the two of us had stayed in touch over the months since I quit treatment at the clinic. Bernie liked reading my stuff, especially my stories. As a favor he even submitted one of my longer pieces to a story editor guy he knew at an independent film company. When he phoned, we would talk about writing and from time to time he dropped over for coffee. Kerri was fond of him too and had a couple of his CDs, even though she wasn't much of a blues fan. Bernie was always smart enough not to show up at our place drunk or on the juice.

That night on the phone he invited us to a party. Bernie said it would be the hoot of the year. Mae West's eighty-fifth-birthday bash benefit was being held at the Beverly Wilshire Hotel, and Bernie himself was playing lead horn in the band. The tickets were free to the musicians and their families and so was the catered dinner.

Kerri and I rented one of the black Lincoln Town Cars and a driver from my cab company, and we showed up in style. It had been seventy-four days and I still hadn't had a drink.

My pretty black-haired girlfriend loved glitz and when Mae herself made an entrance and the band played "Hey, Big Spender," everybody cheered and went nuts. The old broad sashayed across the floor in her white dress with two young cats carrying the train. I had never seen Mae West in person and was taken aback by her size. This big star was no more than five feet tall. Her white stacked hair and high heels made her a foot bigger. To me she looked pitiable. A wrinkled, Fellini-movie cartoon character. The whole deal was a bizarre sideshow.

All the fluff and pretentiousness began to piss me off and

make me nervous. I hated weddings and social events and always felt awkward when I had to make phony chitchat with slick, Hollywood-type, know-it-all jerks.

Booze was everywhere. There was an open bar and the hotel had even provided a crew of guys carrying silver trays. They weaved through the crowd loaded down with champagne and everything else anyone could want. Even vodka and tonic—my former drink of choice. On a band break, when "B" came over to say hello, he was pretty sloshed. He gave Kerri a clumsy kiss and ogled her tanned tits. Then he grabbed her arm and pulled her off to meet his old lady Jeannie one of the backup singers.

A stuffed shirt in an expensive suit was standing near me pontificating about Cary Grant and Frank Capra and the fucking golden age in Hollywood. I was a fish out of water and about ready to inject a comment pertaining to his toupee and stupidity when the drink tray came floating by.

Without a second thought I halted the waiter and grabbed a tall, clear one that contained a wedge of lime. The first sip was toxic as hell. My mouth filled with liquid charcoal. My reaction was to spit the stuff back in the glass.

I waited half a minute, looking around to see if my girlfriend was stalking me, then tried again. The taste was the same. Awful. But this time I didn't have to spit it out.

A minute later I took a big sip, almost a gulp, and swallowed. Better.

Kerri was gone long enough for me to down several more drinks and by the end of the night my allergy to alcohol had diminished to zero.

The next day was Saturday. I was in the 99 Cents Only Store on Sunset Boulevard with a bad hangover and the Yellow Pages in one hand and twenty quarters in the other, going down the list calling rooming houses for weekly prices. I had just been given the heave-ho by Kerri for the final time.

The manager guy at the Ocean Park Hotel in Santa Monica

quoted me $187 per week for a room. Bathrooms weren't private. The men's floor, he said, had a communal-type locker room set up with showers, but each of the small single apartments had a TV, a microwave, and a sink. During World War II the hotel had been the employee quarters for Hughes Aircraft's out-of-town line assembly mechanics.

I made a reservation with the guy to come by in an hour. On the way along Sunset, I stopped at Consumer's Liquor for a short dog to even me out.

The breakup with my girlfriend was inevitable, I told myself; it was just a matter of time anyway. Too much water under the bridge.

Returning to my old Pontiac after the liquor store and buying an *L.A. Times*, I climbed in and cracked my short dog. I took a long blast before starting the car.

Continuing west on Sunset, I began reflecting back over the relationship. There was one thing I considered lucky. It had saved my ass at the time, temporarily at least. It was me cautioning Kerri to wait and not get another dog. Remembering when she made the suggestion sent a jolt of electricity up my spine. A new dog in the house surely would have blown it for me. No telling what the mutt would find while nosing around in the garden near the child-sized dirt mound behind the hedge.

Caveat Emptor

FOR ONCE THE FIRING squad in my head was quiet. The result of three hours of solid sleep and no hangover. It was 5:30 a.m. Just dawn. The long bus ride from Mar Vista to my taxi garage near La Cienega Boulevard had been made easier by revisiting a thin volume of e.e. cummings's early poetry.

It was mid-December in L.A., a hot spell of Santa Ana winds off the desert. Already seventy-five degrees at street level. By seven o'clock that night, I would lose another five to seven pounds of sweat. Twelve hours on the seat grinding out a living in my unair-conditioned cab.

I picked up my trip sheet and found #627 parked in the sea of yellow in the lot next to the taxi dispatch office. For once, the inside of the rear passenger area was fairly clean. Whoever had driven the cab on the last shift had had a slow night.

Rolling all the windows down, I started the car. So far, so good. No clunking in the engine or screeching fan belt noises. I checked the radiator and the oil dipstick. They were both okay.

Inside the cab, behind the wheel, my next order of business was to copy the odometer mileage on the top of my trip sheet in the slot provided. I read the numbers off the dash and wrote them in the green box on the card: 94,261. #627 had been a new Dodge taxi thirteen months ago. These days it gasped and pinged and needed work twice a week.

It was now fully daylight. The blazing orange fireball above the Bonaventure Hotel was working its way up between the tenements in East Hollywood. My boom box was on the seat next to me, beside my poetry notebook and my cummings paperback. I clicked the ON button, then dialed to the all-news station to get the day's forecasts: ninety to ninety-three degrees. Smoggy. Forcing #627's gearshift down into D, I punched the gas pedal.

In five minutes, I was up La Cienega and crossing Wilshire on my way to Beverly Hills, where the fast money is early in the day. My two daily steadies, both downtown financial guys, weren't due for their pickups until after eight o'clock, so I was in the hunt for my first fare. With no one hailing me, I turned east on Santa Monica Boulevard. That's when I saw her.

Being an L.A. cabby requires a highly tuned sense of danger. Vibes and street smarts are everything. After several years of hacking off and on, after being held up and knifed, I was no exception. The woman on the curb looked okay. No problem. In her late twenties, Mexican or European, lipsticked, and dressed in a maroon warm-up outfit. Her dyed-blonde hair was combed straight back and tied with a ribbon. But there was something else as she got in and recited her destination. It may have been her smile, or the way she said the words with the trace of a Latino accent. Something genuine and open. Special. For me, a guy always on his guard against people, a guy who spent his days and nights alone as much as possible, drinking and reading and typing, or just drinking, it felt like I had walked into a flower shop for the first time.

I make it an imperative to say as little as possible to passengers, but a conversation started anyway. The name tag on her jacket spelled out LESLEE. I learned that she was a massage therapist at Blow Up, a high-rent gym on Melrose Avenue, and a college-dropout art major. Born and raised in Boyle Heights.

When we got to the address on Melrose and she paid her fare, her smile filled the back of my cab. "Thanks," she said, swinging the door open; "jou're a nice guy, Bruno. Hab a wonda-ful gooo day. I mean it toooo."

"Ditto," my inarticulate idiot mouth replied. "You do the same." Then she was gone.

As it turned out, the next day was a repeat of the first, only ten minutes later in the morning. I had gotten a slow start because #627 needed a gallon of green radiator coolant. On my way up La Cienega, after no one hailed me, I again turned east on Santa Monica Boulevard. There was Leslee. This time she looked rushed. But the smile was there like the sweet blast of air-conditioning. "Hi, Brunesimo," she said, in her wispy, south-of-the-border accent, remembering my name. "Wha a nice surprise. Goo to zee jou." I nodded and tried my best to return the smile.

"Koo jou hurry up? I'm late. I been burnin' my cannel ah bot ens."

This time my unsophisticated yap did better. A hip, literary answer, courtesy of Edna St. Vincent Millay herself. "Oh," says I, quoting: 'Your candle burns at both ends . . . it will not last the night . . . But ah, your foes, and oh, your friends, it gives a lovely light.'

Her smile back said it all.

Leslee's first massage client of the day would be an intense Beverly Hills CEO who arrived at 6:15 sharp every morning. A hundred bucks plus tip. She wanted to know if I would be willing to pick her up on a daily basis so she wouldn't have to worry about being late for the guy and calling cab companies so early in the morning. "Okay. Sure. No problem," I said eagerly. "That's fine. I'd like that."

So that's the way we began. That first, deep puncture of the ice pick.

Slowly, I began to open up to her. It was tough for me, this sudden, clumsy candidness. But by week's end, after a coffee date in our free time and a couple of long phone conversations about who and how rich her massage clients were, and her wanting to see my poetry and me viewing two books of her drawings, eventually, rebelling against my own prescribed isolation, weary of vodka and porno videos and my seething, genocidal thoughts, I convinced myself that I might somehow be starting to care about somebody else.

Then, on Friday, a clammy, drizzling Los Angeles morning, as I was dropping Leslee off, she leaned forward across the back of my seat to pay, as usual, and I got a surprise. A kiss. A firm, determined tongue forced itself between my lips, then withdrew quickly. "I been wantin' to do tha all week," she said breathlessly.

"Me too," my throat croaked.

Soon after that came the time, the only time as it turned out, that we made it. It was in my cab. That, too, was another ad-lib surprise. I had picked her up from work at five o'clock and we were heading west on 3rd Street in the heavy rush-hour traffic. "Hey," she whispered, "jou wanna see somethin'? I been keeping it kool for jou."

At the next red light, I turned and looked back over the seat. My passenger was naked from the waist down in the bumper-to-bumper traffic. Shaved pink crotch. Legs apart, wearing her beaming, million-peso grin.

I should have known. The flashing orange caution light going off in my brain was delivering a steady message: *This Is All Too Easy . . . Something's Wrong . . .* But, in truth, in hindsight, I knew I was lost. Nothing else but that wondrous thing resting itself lovingly on the vinyl of my back seat mattered. I had never gotten it on with anyone in a cab in open daylight before. Between parked cars.

It was the following Monday that I had my first symptoms. A redness between my legs. An itching. Then a blotch in my pubic hair that by the end of the day was a dime-sized sore.

When I mentioned my problem to Leslee on our ride the

next day, her response was blasé. No big deal. Whatever it was would go away. Then the smile. The no prisoners—gimme all your cash and credit cards—I love you forever—smile.

Two days later my herpes sore was in full blossom, oozing and burning like mad. My cab company's fat HMO witch doctor took one look and diagnosed the condition immediately. Along with his free medical opinion came a stern warning to ease up on the juice, a flash of brilliance I'd put together for myself years earlier.

Leslee denied everything, then unaccountably disappeared.

By the end of the following week, when none of my phone calls were returned and she was a steady no-show on the corner of Santa Monica Boulevard in the morning, I took matters into my own hands, stopping by her gym after parking #627 at a meter on a side street a block away.

The desk guy at Blow Up eyed me up and down as I walked in. He was muscular and smiling, an iron-pumping geek. Intentionally unhelpful and acting busy. He'd pegged me as a slob in blue jeans and a drip-dry shirt. A nonperson in Hollywood.

Finally, after two requests, I got louder. It was then that he buzzed into the massage area from the switchboard intercom. After he hung up, the George Clooney charm was back. He eyed me up and down again and announced: "Leslee is presently occupied with a client."

I had all day, I said. I would wait.

So for the next hour, I sat in one of the expensive gray leather chairs outside the spa area keeping my eyes on the little window in the massage-room door. Finally, a guy in a towel from the male exercise area sat down next to me. "Who you waiting for?" he whispered. "Which girl?"

"Leslee," I said.

"Hey, me too. Jesus! Shit! Maybe she double-booked herself!"

"I don't have an appointment," I said.

His eyes narrowed, then he snickered. "Well," he said, "you'd better sign up and get in line from now on. You won't be sorry.

For an extra fifty she'll give you the whole deal, the total-body massage. And for fifty more, what do you think you get?"

"I already know," I said.

Marble Man

I WAS TELEMARKETING, SLAMMING unsuspecting mooch-es. Talking them into buying oil and gas leases from a tele-phone boiler room on Santa Monica Boulevard in Hollywood. A great scam. I'd needed a break from taxi driving, and phone room work gave me more time to write. The money I made was keeping me well stocked in gin and amphetamines. At night I wrote poetry and set my goal at a poem a day. Do or die.

My boss, Milt, and his wife, a beautiful, twenty-five-year-old smart-mouthed brat from Beverly Hills, were trying to rent an apartment close to work in town so they wouldn't have to com-mute three hours a day up and down the Ventura Freeway from Thousand Oaks. One afternoon Milt was busy doing job interviews and asked me to accompany blonde, silicone-titted Irene to look at a potential sublet in Marina del Rey.

It was a top-floor penthouse, a move-in, take-over-the-rent, furniture and all, deal. Expensive for a two bedroom. $3,500 a month.

The renters' names were Donald and Kate. Don was being transferred to Silicon Valley. A computer guy. Just before Don and Kate found out about his transfer, they had completed re-modeling their twenty-square-foot bathroom. Elegant, expen-sive shit. New faucets, flashy chrome-and-glass shower, new sink, mahogany cabinets, and several big blocks of polished red marble inside the tub that extended out to fill half the room. Don himself had helped the contractor with the carpentry and build-out modifications.

To get there, Irene ordered us a limo. Chain-smoking Sherman cigarettes, the bitch gave orders to everybody, employees, husbands, chauffeurs, and cabbies alike. "Hey," she snapped, "turn here . . ." "I'm late, okay? Do the letters T-I-P mean anything to you?" That shit.

As she sat in the backseat, squirming around, her white slacks were tight enough for me to count her pubic hairs through the material.

It was midafternoon when we arrived to look at the place. Don and Kate were halfway down a bottle of tequila. Don was a tall bald Black man. Well educated. Six-five or six-six and very formal in manner and speech. His contact lenses made him blink continuously. Kate was long-legged and pretty with a mini skirt and dark eyeliner and white/blonde, Madonna-style hair. Her capped teeth were perfect too.

The man of the house was online on his computer doing business when we came in, so Kate—well buzzed on her tequila and Coke—showed us the kitchen, then the bedrooms with the view of Santa Monica Bay, then the closet space. When we came to the master bathroom, she giggled and whispered to Irene, "Don't mind Donald. He has this thing for marble. See?" She pushed the door open and there it was, like a movie set or a glitzy photograph out of an interior designer catalog. The room might have been the ornate crapper in the presidential suite at the Beverly Wilshire. Kate turned on the shower to demonstrate. Spray popped out from eight jets in the walls.

Irene, for once turning on the charm, went crazy touching fixtures and overreacting. Then, trying to impress Kate, she started blabbing about her extensive personal knowledge of marble. Was the marble in Kate's bathroom Bolivian? From La Paz? Did Kate know that the best marble came from Bolivia?

Kate's marble was domestic, from Arkansas. Kate had never heard of marble coming from Bolivia.

After the bathroom, down a long hall of antique photographs of Sunset Boulevard in the 1920s that Irene made a point of admiring and oozing over, Kate was about to show us the half bath when Donald joined in, handing out strong tequila and Cokes to me and my boss's wife.

Don was as drunk as Kate, so when Irene opened her mouth to kiss his ass about their elegant decorative toilet modifications, he couldn't resist dragging us back down the hall to reintroduce us to the stupid bathroom.

I sat on the edge of the tub while Don went into a five-minute pitch about the evolution of marble from crystalline limestone and the right way a surface should be prepared to "receive" a fitted marble section. Don let us know that he personally polished his bathroom once a week. Were we aware that marble was porous? I wasn't, but braless Irene was. As it turned out, Irene was an authority on Bolivian marble and every other fucking thing.

According to Kate, I looked exactly like Larry-somebody, a motocross champion she knew at USC's School of Dentistry.

I got restless, finished my glass, and got up to escape from the conversation. I asked Kate for another drink, and said I wanted to see the ocean view from the living room. Nothing doing. Donald motioned for Kate to get us all a refill. While she was in the kitchen pouring tequila, Don began running his eyes over my boss's wife's body and wanting to know if Irene was into aerobics because she was so slim. I knew Irene's formula for weight loss—it was the same as her husband's and mine—a gram of cocaine a day.

Donald opened a cabinet. In it were a dozen labeled and polished samples of marble. Different colors. Some from Arkansas and some from Carrera, Italy. A chunk or two from Spain. None from fucking Bolivia. Don began touching and fondling these rocks and wanted me to hold each one and experience its texture. When Don got excited about things, he tended to blink and squint nonstop. After he handed me each sample, I passed the moron shit on to Irene.

Kate came back with the drinks, gave one to everybody, then strolled over to the toilet, pulled her dress up and her panties down, and had a pee while Don and my boss's wife discussed bathroom accessories and marble and grout and porousness.

Donald was now continually leering at Irene's tits and crotch. He changed the subject to carpentry. Fittings. Tongue and groove. His nail drawer.

Kate wanted to know if I knew what an outstanding carpenter Donald was. Before I could nod or say anything, Irene interjected about how much she loved carpentry. Her cousin Spencer, president of his own accounting firm on Beverly Boulevard and the owner of the entire building, had built the office lobby tables at his company in his spare time.

It was getting hot in the bathroom and Donald wanted to know if any of us minded him taking off his shirt.

Nobody minded.

Kate went to a wall unit. It had a special wide nail drawer. She opened it slowly as if it contained a museum exhibit of fossilized ostrich eggs. The inside was spotless, lined with taped-down butcher paper. There were two dozen types of nails. Each type had its own divided section. Everything perfectly arranged in shiny, clear plastic, see-through holders.

Clearly, Kate found this shit fascinating. Especially the larger, thicker nails. She held up a few of the plastic containers. Opening one, she slid several thick ones into my hand. I checked them out, rolled them around, felt the points, then gave them back. Then she passed them over to Irene, who acted inspired and privileged to be permitted to touch them.

The pigsnot conversation circulating in the bathroom was becoming too much.

There were hammers in another drawer. Three kinds, a ball peen, a claw, and a smaller finishing-nail hammer. All perfect looking and unused, gleaming, with thick black rubber grips.

Kate removed the big claw hammer the way a surgeon picks up a scalpel from an operating tray. She could tell by my face that I didn't give a fuck any more about hammers or any of it, so she passed them to Irene directly.

Then, back sitting on the toilet with the seat down and her panties showing between her legs, Kate asked Irene if she considered herself to be a sexual person. Irene squirmed, adjusted her skintight slacks, but nodded yes.

Kate was smiling and fondling the handle of the claw hammer. Had Irene ever had sex with a Black man? A real, full-on amazing Black lover?

That was enough for me. I went bottoms up with my new drink and wanted another. Since Donald and Kate were so friendly about tequila and involved with Irene, I got up myself and slipped out to the kitchen.

I took my time and fixed a nice one. More tequila than Coke. They had a hefty glass jar of raisins and nuts, so I ate some of those, too.

When I came back, Donald was naked and getting into the shower to give Irene a demonstration of how the eight simultaneous water jets operated. The girls were sharing space on the toilet seat, watching.

I had never seen a dick as big as Donald's dick. It looked more like someone's extra arm than a cock. But I had no interest at all in Kate or Donald or his bathing habits or his porous marble or his nail drawer. I asked my boss's wife if she minded me leaving and going back to Hollywood without her. Irene took a big sip off my drink, smiled benignly, and said it was fine for me to leave. She was going to hang around and see the rest of the apartment.

THE NEXT DAY, AT work on a break, I asked Irene if she had decided to sublet the place.

She was hungover, smoking a cigarette, and in a lousy mood.

"Pass," she hissed. "Rent's too high. And the view? Who gives a shit about Santa Monica Pier?"

Then she squashed the cigarette under a white, knee-high boot and started to walk back inside.

"I thought you liked the marble," I said.

Irene glared. "Arkansas marble is domestic ca-ca. Gar-bahje. Those two know squat about marble. Didn't I tell them nothing compares to Bolivian marble? Remember?"

"Sure. I remember," I said.

"Then stop asking me stupid questions."

Princess

LIBBY IS A NUT. From the first day I met the guy he was prone to excess and outrageousness. The name Libby is short for Liberation; I still don't know his real name. He is tall, well over six feet, even without his boots, and one of his top front teeth is missing. When I first met him, he weighed no more than a hundred and fifty pounds and his most unsettling characteristics—other than his height and the missing tooth— were his propensity to never shut up and the nearly constant public use of the words *fuck* and *cocksucker*. Scandalizing the proletariat has always been the main way Libby got his kicks. Even now.

On the day we met, he struck me as a beat-up, blabber-mouth rock star—an alumnus of the Keith Richards school of beauty. He hadn't slept in twenty-four hours, and his dirty, shoulder-length black hair was cut in a Mohawk style with the top brush area dyed red. That day his wardrobe consist- ed of a wrinkled black shirt and leather pants and snakeskin boots. The boots appeared to have been hurriedly painted pink to complement his hair.

The first time was by accident. Either he or his girlfriend, who answered to the name Bitch, had telephoned my taxi company's 800 number to hire a cab to take their remaining bedroom boxes from an apartment in Venice to their house on the side of a hill, overlooking the coastline, in Malibu. The dispatcher's radio call came to me because my taxi was the closest car to the address, on Ozone Court. For me, in those days, staying sober and uncrazy was a major challenge. To keep on writing, I worked three or four shifts a week as a cab driver. My mental disposition would not permit more.

Sometimes good things happen to people here in L.A. and Liberation is one of those guys who got lucky in the movie business. Perhaps, after seeing him face-to-face in his rock star getup, that film producer decided Libby somehow looked the part of a production designer. According to Liberation, who twists the truth at will, the man hired him on the spot after viewing his dazzling portfolio of masterful sketches. Before that, Libby worked for ten years as a grunt draftsman in downtown L.A. in the Design Mart. However it happened, the movie job worked out well. The film won a festival prize and eventually became a financial success. Another movie assignment followed that one. And so on. So, by the time we met in my cab that day, Liberation was on a roll and the large Hollywood paychecks were permitting him numerous bad habits and excesses.

After we loaded his boxes into my cab, I discovered right away that my passenger and his girlfriend were no strangers to the booze and drug scene of Venice. While we drove up the coast in the direction of Malibu Pier, with Bitch following in their restored '58 Buick Roadmaster convertible, hauling additional boxes, Libby continued to yak manically and filled my nose from a gram vial of coke while we passed an open quart of VO across the seat back.

Somewhere on the ride, he must have decided that they would need the use of me and my taxi for the entire afternoon. Because when we arrived at the three-story house that extended off the side of a hill on stilts, my passenger stuffed a roll of ten twenty-dollar bills into my hand. The money easily covered my pay for the shift. I said thanks as I shoved the cash in my pocket, and after that we began carrying their load up the stairs to the master bedroom.

The inside of the house looked like a dingy West Hollywood art gallery. The walls and rugs and furniture had once been all white and the living room was covered with Libby's wild, floor-to-ceiling framed original designs.

As the work continued, Bitch, barefoot, dressed in her jeans and T-shirt, began making separate trips up and down from the kitchen with drinks and a fresh vial of white, top-grade, Colombian Marching Powder. Like a ghost, Bitch would appear quietly in the doorway. Smiling. She was not a talker but in her way a good person. Always friendly. I was having a busman's holiday. Happy as a pig in poop.

The entire unpacking task might easily have been accomplished in ordinary time but Liberation, as I said, was a ringmaster of endless bullshit. Our work kept getting sidetracked by his riffs on topics like American political corruption and the Trilateral Commission, and Israeli terrorism. And citizens rights. And the IRS. "Man, didja know that there are only two major economic powers in the world that don't have nationalized health care? Who are these cocksuckers, you ask? Well, for one: those racist fucking assholes from South Africa. And for two: the good old cocksuckin', George Bush, U S of A."

"No kidding," I heard myself say, squeezing in the words. "I don't have health insurance."

Liberation sneered. "Exactly my point, ace. Exactly. Precise-a-fuckin'-mundo."

Along with his political declarations, the guy with the pink hair enjoyed dishing gossip about folks he had worked with in the film business. There was the actress who while drunk had given her seventeen-year-old kid a blowjob in the hot tub by mistake. "Ha! Ha! Imagine finding out that you just let your own fuckin' son squirt his load down your throat. Uhhhhhh!"

And there was the director guy who used to do kiddie porn

in Van Nuys before he began making movies with Michelle Pfeiffer. Liberation had no love for this cat, and while they worked together on the set, Libby made it his job to clip out provocative photographs of preteens twice a week, then anonymously tack the pictures to the film crew's Call Board.

At the back end of each harangue, my benefactor would laugh his crazy laugh that flashed the hole in his teeth, then launch into a new topic. His yakking never stopped.

Eventually, I learned that we both had used the services of the same drug dealer at the Sunset Cuzoon. A bad-smelling fat asshole named B. B. Bowman. And we both knew Slavin' Dave, the guitar player whose band gave the free concerts on Sundays at the Sidewalk Café on Venice Beach.

After about a third of the unpacking had been done, it became apparent that the only items in the pile of stacked boxes were pairs of Libby's boots. In total, fifty-five sets of boots. He would pass me a pair, interrupt whatever monologue he was on, and say something like: "Hey, check these out, my man. These are Borghese, from Milano. Handmade. Eleven hundred bucks." Or, "I got these cocksuckers in Argentina. Feel the leather."

I would oblige, examine the boots, then slide them into the closet with the others. Everything was expensive and, according to my host, all custom-made.

By the time the job was done, we were quite drunk and high from snorting coke, but the long hardwood floor of the bedroom closet was neatly lined end to end with exotic footwear.

A fresh glass of VO in one hand, flashing his trailer-park grin, Liberation commanded that I follow him down the stairs. "C'mon, my man," he said, rolling his eyes, brushing past Bitch, "I want to show you something. It'll make your dick stand up like a cocksucking cruise missile. No shit."

"Sure," I said, grabbing my own drink, then wobbling after him out of the bedroom. "Let's do it."

Arriving at the basement after three flights, Libby stuck a

special-looking key into the door's brass tumbler, then pushed it open.

Inside, there was no furniture at all, and the walls were made entirely of glass on three sides, but the most noticeable thing in the room was the abrupt change in temperature. It was airless inside, heavy and wet and at least thirty degrees hotter than anywhere else in the house. Pinkboots bolted the door behind us and slipped the key into his pants pocket.

Tree trunks and heavy branches crisscrossed the open area, and a layer of straw covered the tiled floor. The place appeared to be a do-it-yourself zoo cage. Possibly an enclosure for wild dogs or monkeys or a bear. But even drunk, I didn't like being in the room. I don't like cages. At all.

Libby began clapping and whistling and stomping his foot. He kept this up for half a minute, but nothing changed. Then he repeated the process. He was grinning again, but this time when I observed the black gap in his mouth, I felt impending trouble. His expression was that of a salivating perv whacking off to a porn video. And the information being conveyed to me from my booze-soaked brain wasn't good either. Maybe, I thought, this skinny, chattering, toothless nutjob was about to permit my ass to get attacked by whatever he kept in this cage. Perhaps I had been lured here by Jesus to finally get my comeuppance, locked down with a satanic prankster and a crocodile, or a huge rodent or some horrific, carnivorous, cab-driver-eating beastfuck.

Finally, there was movement in the far corner of the room, and a large section of the floor began to shift and reshape itself. A few seconds later Princess's head popped up above the straw and she slowly began advancing across a dead branch.

I had not been within six feet of any kind of snake for years. In fact, as a kid living near open fields, in the summer, when my big brother, Nick, would surprise me at night by having two or three lizards or a king snake in bed with us in the dark, I had developed a distinct hatred toward all things that slither.

Libby began rattling off Princess's statistics: The monster was a Burmese python. She was eighteen feet long and eight inches thick, with a weight somewhere around six hundred pounds. He explained that Princess had once belonged to Bitch's father, a rich agronomist guy who traveled around the world irrigating the desert and teaching backward nations how to grow food in unusable dirt. The house we were in had belonged to Dad, too. Bitch's Pops, before his undescribed death, had deeded the place to her. The care and feeding of Princess was rolled in as part of the deal.

Blab, blab, blab. There was more. Relationship data snot about how Libby and Bitch had gotten together, about how he had been overcome by the weirdness of his karma and good fortune at hooking up with a soul mate who admired serpents as much as he did. Aleister Crowley-type demonic, sick, creepiness shit.

I hated all of it. What Bitch had inherited. How they got together. All of it. This chattering asshole required immediate murdering. My imperative was to silence his mouth for ten seconds, in order to allow my mind to calculate a way to break a window or steal the key to get out of the cage. Meanwhile, it was becoming clear that the huge animal scooching up the log in my direction wasn't at all inhibited by shyness.

Backing my body toward the door, I watched as the snake finally coasted to the top of her stump a few feet away. Happily there, the giant fucker began twisting itself around the log.

Liberation's face was at eye level to Princess and no more than three feet away when she began to whip her long, split tongue in and out.

"Hey look, she's hungry," giggled the eerie scarecrow who hadn't slept in thirty-six hours.

"No kidding?" I said, now aware of two black eyes being fixed on me—sizing me up. "Look, friend, I don't like snakes. And this is a very big snake."

The zookeeper sneered. "That's okay, my man. It's easy to fucking see that you don't know shit one about vipers. For your information these cocksuckers only eat what they can get their jaws around. Pythons don't bite. They don't have teeth. They swallow."

"I'll say it another way: I don't want to be here. Give me the key. Let me out."

Liberation's attention span for other people's issues was limited, and he had become distracted by petting his snake.

I stayed glued against the door until he finally spun around in my direction. "C'mon, man," he barked, "let's go get our baby some food. She hasn't eaten in three or four days."

Cross Creek Shopping Center was ten minutes north on the Coast Highway. Planck's Pet & Feed is one of the storefronts in the long line of high-end boutique shops. The girl behind the counter recognized her tall, steady customer as he entered the shop, and obligingly began folding together several new air-holed pet boxes.

Captain Blabbermouth got right down to business. He gestured at the cages lining the side counters. "I'll take a dozen of the bunnies," he demanded. "Those little fuckers too," he said, stabbing his finger in the direction of the wire coops containing rats of differing color patterns. "How many have you got?"

The kid in the blue apron was unsure. "I don't know. A dozen and a half, or twenty," she said. "How many do you want?"

Liberation was groping in his pocket for his bankroll. "Fuck it. Bag 'em all. The more the merrier," he said, flashing his gapped smile.

He was counting out money by the register when he spied a good-sized brown animal caged in a corner near the front door. "What's that?" he asked the girl. "What kinda fat-rat cocksucker is that?"

The kid didn't blink. "That's not a rat, sir. That's a possum. We received our first pair last week. A brother and sister. They make excellent pets but they're quite shy."

"Him too," Libby hissed. "But we'll need a separate box for mister porky possum." Then he leaned toward me. "Spare parts," he whispered. "An extra tasty treat for my Princess."

"Have you got a carton big enough?"

"Of course," said the girl.

"Cool. Box him up."

But I'd had enough. After we returned to the cliff house inhabited by the mute black chick and the snake, I was done, pissed off, completely sober, and sickened by the knowledge of what was to come.

I helped Libby finish carting the boxes of live food down the stairs, stacking them against the cage door, then I faced him. He could see by my expression that I had gone as far as I was willing to go. Clearly, I wasn't interested in hanging around to watch Princess do her act.

He didn't look surprised. "Okay, my man," he said with a grin. He extended his hand, "Thaz cool. Thanks for the help . . . Hey, you okay?"

"I am now, you crazy whackjob fucker."

TWO YEARS PASSED. MAYBE three. I sobered up intermittently, wrote half a novel and threw it out, did a twenty-eight-day bit in a psych ward, and eventually found myself in an out-patient recovery program that convened twice a week. With the exception of my mind, I was doing okay, living back in Venice, and driving for a private car service. But one night I had a slip and got drunk and sliced my wrist in a blackout. The ambulance came and transported me as a 51/50 to the emergency room at Brotmann's Hospital. Three days later they placed me at SOBER (Self-help Obtained by Enlightened Recovery), a dry-out deal in Culver City.

There were four men to a room. We had group therapy twice a day and private evaluation sessions with the shrink, Dr. Tomasso, once each week.

One night, after lights out, I heard conversation in the next dorm. In fact, it wasn't two people talking but a single voice, a jerk who wouldn't shut up.

Because of my history of "clean" time, I had been made a night trustee. My job was to keep order after lights out in the dorms and snitch on all wrongdoers to the a.m. administrator. The compensation for being a trustee is unlimited access to the padlocked cafeteria refrigerator and real coffee.

Getting out of bed, I went next door to inform the trouble-maker that he was violating Ward Rule 7 on the poster tacked to the big board in the hallway. Of course, when I opened the door, there was Liberation sitting on his cot, upright like a used ice-cream stick, joyously pissing off his bunkmates.

It was his first night at SOBER. I shook his hand and said hello, but I knew right away by his expression that he couldn't place me.

The brother in the bed next to Libby's suggested that since we were acquainted, I might want to take his skinny, yakking white-boy ass down the hall to the cafeteria and calm him down. If not, he had no problem going over my head to the night orderly, who would issue Warning Number 1 on the way to getting Libby kicked out.

The tall man on the cot was even more gaunt and weary-look-ing than I remembered. In those days the new style was skin-head and Libby was now punked out, shaved completely bald, with a row of a dozen silver earrings and a pierced lip. Some-time in the last couple of years, he had added a long tattoo of a snake. It wound around his right arm from the top to the wrist. The bags under his eyes had become permanent, and his miss-ing tooth had been replaced by a set of the kind fitted to order.

In the dark, we drank the rotting herbal tea dispensed 24/7 at the cafeteria while I filled him in on the events of our first meeting. He couldn't remember about me or my cab or our trip to the pet store for Princess. That was okay. A natural brain fart, considering the circumstances.

When I was done talking, SOBER's new inpatient became oddly speechless. It was as if my words had cast a spell of silence. For half a minute he just sat in his chair, staring past the tables in the unlighted room. Finally, he jerked one of my cigarettes from the open pack on the table and lit it. "That bitch!" he yowled. "That cocksucking fucking cunt liar bitch."

With that he was off. My memoir had touched a flame to a gas main. For the next hour all I needed to do was be there in the dark. Breathing in and out.

No happy endings here. It turned out that within a few months after I was introduced to Princess, Libby and Bitch had gone on to discover speedballing and shooting smack as a pastime.

At first, with his income, they could almost afford the ride. But after a while it turned into a daily deal. Junkies all tell me that heroin is for people who love themselves but in truth, almost no one can handle the freight. Over time, invariably, slamming shit will have the effect of relocating one's possessions. Work ethic and cash flow become seriously fucked. And the more he and Bitch dabbled, the more unimportant his movie deadlines became. It took a year for them to run through his film money and for Libby to become a repeated no-show at important production meetings. "Man, bro, no shit; one or two mistakes and the cocksuckers dumped my fucking ass like a stepchild. Kno wh'am sayin'?"

I knew.

After that, rather than make any lifestyle course correction, the couple elected to hock the cliff house. "Hey, ya gotta do what ya gotta do. Am I right?"

"First things first," I said, sliding in the words. Sipping my tea.

The mortgage of the house brought in an immediate windfall. In those days, homes in Malibu like Bitch's place on the hill above the ocean were selling for upwards of $500,000, so the couple's problems were solved for the time being. Sort of. Libby kept the faith and continued to assure his girlfriend that a new movie gig would show up any day. But producers and production designers and movie editors all know that once you've blown your reputation in Hollywood, chance two almost never comes.

After a six-month visit to Milano, where Liberation explored designer possibilities, and another six in heroin-rich Amsterdam on an extended vacation, the couple were back at the hocked cliff house with most of their money spent. To supplement their smack habit, Libby now sold dope.

But there was still the problem of the stupid snake. Once back at home, the expenditure of $500 a week for live food for Princess had become decidedly excessive as weighed against the cost of two days' worth of heroin. An overindulgence. Rather than murder and wall-mount the malevolent fucker or donate it to be ground up and sold as plant-food mulch, Libby devised a plan to supply his creature with living red-meat food and avoid the cash drain.

The grin was back. Across the cafeteria table in the darkness, the skinhead with the earrings was giggling at his own weirdness, looking smug, showing no signs of fatigue whatever. He'd already smoked half my cigarettes and consumed five cups of the rancid herbal tea.

"So, where's the goddamn snake now?" I asked, eyes watering, exhausted, trying to cut to the chase.

"Well, the cocksucker was eating us out of house and home, like I'm sayin'. But to me giving Princess up would have been equal to giving up ... like ... a kind of legacy. And I wasn't going to do that to our baby, even though if I knew then what I know now, how my lyin' twat cocksucker girlfriend was gonna dime me out to the law an' all, I mighta done the whole thing different. Whothefuck knows, ya know?"

"Okay."

"Cocksucker! Bitch twat cocksucker! Fucking treacherous poisonous cunt slut!"

I pushed my chair back. "Look," I said, "I'm going to sleep. We'll finish this up in the morning. If you don't want to get eighty-sixed from the program, just remember to keep quiet in the dorm. Violation of the talking rule is grounds for discharge. The first buzzer goes off at 5:30."

"Fuck that! No way! Just let me tell it. Completely bizarre shit. You'll love it, I fuckin' promise. You say you're a wannabe writer. Just listen. Totally fucking bizarre."

"I'm tired."

"Five fuckin' minutes, I promise."

"Okay. Deal. Let's hear it."

"Cool. So fuckin' Princess is up to two hundred and fifty pounds a week in food. You know, bunnies and gerbils and lab mice. That shit. And now the cocksucker's twenty feet long and weighs Christ knows how much. Right?"

"Right."

Then, like a spewing gusher of undigested vomit, it came out. Libby, in full voice, commenced detailing his atrocities in the name of the murderous, overindulged python. It was sick stuff. Mayhem and sadism. His polluting tale engulfed the darkened cafeteria like great chunks of unprocessed municipal turds after a Santa Monica Bay rainstorm. The account exceeded every twisted nutjob limit of the most strange and creeped-out grotesque dope-fiend diabolical perversity.

Here's an accurate summary, omitting, of course, the use of the words *cocksucker* and *fuck* eleven thousand times. And also shortened by half an hour: In L.A. there are several throwaway newspapers where citizens place free or low-cost ads for their used stuff. Mostly it's junk. Secondhand bikes and TVs and out-of-date computers and CD players. Garage-type merchandise. But, as it turns out, most all these bargain sheets also contain a section for pet adoptions. One afternoon, while zoned on China White, Liberation is reading his free *Westside Penny Saver* and seizes upon a solution to feed Princess: "FREE PUPPIES. SHEPHERD PUPPIES. SHEPHERD/COLLIES MIX. 6 TOTAL. FIRST COME, FIRST SERVED." . . . "LITTER OF TABBY KITTENS—WITH SHOTS—TO LOVING HOME."

Twice a week Liberation and Bitch began heading out from

the Malibu cliff house in their '58 Buick convertible, with the shiny chrome dash and massive trunk, to pre-called residences around Southern California.

In the beginning, the couple ran into a bit of resistance. Their first problem was one of appearance, like, for instance, Libby is over one-foot taller than Bitch, and in those days he was still sporting his bright red Mohawk. If their target market was to be families in homes with kids, it would, of necessity, have to exclude Hollywood and Venice and the "liberal" westside of town. It was L.A.'s distant and vast gold mine of middle-class residential communities like Hawthorne, Westchester, Long Beach, and Lakewood that would accommodate Princess's feeding frenzies and blood lust. But in these areas, Libby and Bitch encountered culture shock. Pet donors were mostly white, uptight Republicans and Christian right-wingers. At first sight, these folks tended to become unnerved at the strange couple on their front porch ringing the doorbell. Naturally, Libby and Bitch were always stoned on smack too, so reading road maps and asking directions, and getting lost often took hours. As a result, in the beginning, several of their missions to provide victims for their insatiable viper ended in wrong turns and disappointment.

According to Libby, the presentation issue, at least, was solved effortlessly by a stroke of his genius. They purchased a used garage-type teddy bear for Bitch. She would carry the big fluffy fucker to the front door and hug it tenderly while he did the negotiations. The ploy worked.

The other thing the two had going in their favor was their willingness to adopt all the excess pets at each home. Families who had been overburdened with a litter of ten or twelve yapping mongrel mutts were more than pleased at the notion of getting themselves off the hook in one fell swoop.

The only downside for the doper Samaritans was the copious paraphernalia that always seemed to accompany the transactions. Many of suburbia's guilt-ridden homeowners wanted to leave their discarded animals well equipped. So, the Buick's trunk became the repository of useless shit: bags of dry food and wire pet cages and baskets and quilts and colored bowls of every description. The backseat and floor had plenty of room for the animals themselves but after two or three stops, Libby and Bitch usually had to turn back. Once at home they would dump the extraneous crap in their garage.

Naturally Princess couldn't have been happier. A steady stream of live meat got released into her clutches every three or four days. The ghoul fucker could chomp away at her leisure while the dozen or so frantic animals still uneaten in the cage were losing their sanity and exhausting themselves scurrying back and forth seeking a way out. And every once in a while, there was the added bonus of a full-grown dog being donated to the cause because it bit someone or had behavior problems. Yummy.

Then things gradually came to a head. Over time, the massive accumulation of pet junk in Libby and Bitch's darkened car park began to become a health issue. The couple spent most of their waking hours stoned in front of the TV watching videos. They would sell smack to the occasional dope client who dropped by, but little else. Soon enough their garage was overrun with filthy animal cages and rotting pet food. Thoughtlessly, these items had never been discarded. The crap was mostly confined to the garage, but little by little it began to overflow into the kitchen as their storage needs grew. Of course, this got the attention of cockroaches and all manner of creepie-crawlies. Then there was the stink itself. Curious rodents and the other neighborhood animals began congregating and nesting outside the infested, smelly pad.

The fire department and other public services were contacted by their nosy neighbors. Libby himself was up for any and all confrontations, but Bitch had the remnants of a social conscience. She had lived in the house most of her life and didn't like to have to jive and shuck when the locals began rapping on the front door.

The two junkies began to argue. Naturally, Bitch blamed her red-haired roomie. Money had always been a sore spot between them, and since the mortgage they were perpetually ninety days late on the payments. But that was lightweight compared to these new troubles. She sensed that the hammer was about to come down. Firemen were snooping around. Almost daily, white dudes in suits in unmarked cars parked up the block. Local gardeners and kids on their skateboards had been watching them carrying load after load of live animals from the Buick into the house. It was Libby who was the one with all the bright ideas, and now his keen, whacked-out thinking was about to get the two of them permanently jacked up.

Bitch couldn't take the heat. A day or two later he woke up and she was gone, and with her original restored '58 Buick convertible with the chrome dashboard. Later on, that same afternoon, in a foul doper mood, he opened the front door only to be greeted by a distraught pet donor. She'd changed her mind and called and called their number only to hear their answering machine message. Now she was here to get her Bobo back. Her kids were driving her crazy.

Libby was pissed. Out of patience, he said, "Follow me," then clomped his way down the stairs to the converted basement cage. There, he unlocked the door and pointed to Princess. He suggested to the woman that she ask the big snake what had happened to her goddamn Bobo.

Later on, when the cops arrived, he was pretty sure that it was because of the woman who had run from the house and stumbled down the street screaming. That, he found out, was not the case. It was Bitch who had dropped the dime from a women's shelter in Van Nuys.

It was two in the morning by the time he had finished the story. I was done in. I left Liberation there in the cafeteria with one cigarette in the pack and the admonition not to bother anybody else.

Ten days later I was released from SOBER and went back to my apartment in Venice. I kept my court-ordered end of the bargain and returned twice a week for alumni meetings.

Somehow Libby had managed not to get himself ejected from the hospital program. Doctor Tomasso, rather than terminate his whacko-ass, had come to recognize that he was in the presence of a special case. The doc eventually provided Libby with his own private dorm room and changed policy to allow that on a daily basis he might personally monitor this client's recovery.

Later that month, I was attending an evening group session that fell on the same night as Libby's graduation.

There were eleven guys in total who'd made it through the entire four weeks without bolting or violating the rules to get themselves shipped off to the slammer.

I was in the parking lot smoking and talking shit with an old-time alumnus named Base-pipe Bill when Libby walked out the door. He smiled at me and waved goodbye, then got into the classic red '58 Buick Roadmaster convertible parked at the curb. The pretty black girl behind the wheel tried to kiss him but gave up when he wouldn't stop talking. Instead she punched the gas pedal, then turned left onto Washington Boulevard.

IT'S BEEN QUITE A while but I still see Libby and Bitch around town at nighttime AA meetings. We always say hi and shake hands. Bitch still doesn't talk that much.

But hey, you know, what the hell. It's all ancient history now, right? As it turns out, true love did last forever. At least for them.

Renewal

T HE LIGHT WAS EXTREME. Oppressive. A silent white scream, invading me like a message of terrible vengeance from my unconscious. I tried rolling away from it, but the maneuver was useless. Brilliance was everywhere, consuming my sanity.

I could feel myself sweating, my shirt sticking to me, soaked through.

Realizing something was jabbing me in the back, something thick, I reached for the thing and pulled it forward. An empty wine bottle. Mad Dog 20/20.

There was a smell, too. It was choking me. A repugnant pong that combined with the persistent luminosity to render me fully alert. Now I understood. I was waking up—coming out of a blackout.

Squinting, I looked around: A movie theater. Old. Musty. Insufferably hot.

My head was pounding from the concentration of light, so I closed my eyes to give my brain time to unscramble the images it had collected. It was then that I began to sense another person—a body—near me.

Opening my eyes again, I looked to my right in the direction of the stink. A woman. Dark skinned with long, matted hair, unconscious in the seat next to mine. The odor coming from her was the heaviness of her perfume combined with something else. Sweat? Perhaps booze and puke. Something rancid and terrible.

Shielding my vision with my free arm, twisting my body, I pushed myself upright in the seat. The theater was empty. A movie must have just ended because a guy with a broom a few rows away was sweeping trash from the floor, working his way up the aisle toward my row.

·Seeing that my pants were open, loose and unzipped, I tugged them up and refastened the belt.

Now I began a study of the girl with the awful smell. She had thin legs and was wearing wide gold hoop earrings and a tight black dress. Almost surely a hooker, with the deep-set eyes and hard cheekbones of a daily amphetamine hype. Her short dress was pulled above her hips and the dark nipple of one of her tits was exposed. Something had spilled and dried on her dress and in her hair. Something thick, sticky-looking.

I was having trouble with the rest because my brain was still slogged. The pictures my eyes sent back didn't make sense.

Then I saw. I understood. The girl in the seat next to me wasn't a girl at all. She had a strange and tiny cock.

WHEN I GOT BACK to my place in Venice, the rooms were dark. Turning on the kitchen light, I spooked myself when I came face-to-face with Gomez, my fat, bad-tempered orange cat. He hissed his irritation at my arrival, then jumped down from the warmth of the stove. His getaway dislodged a pot containing something brown that clattered down on the linoleum.

In my bedroom, I took off my clothes in the dark and dumped the crap from my pockets on the dresser. It was then that I noticed the goddamn thing missing. Again! My cab driver permit. I had been back working a taxi job for five months and this was the second time I had lost the laminated fucker.

Had I had sex with the Latino transvestite? Had he/she

sucked my cock while I was in my blackout? Was I now capable of anything, completely, incurably, insane?

Next to my bed, on the floor, were a dozen empty beer bottles. I was seized by the urge to smash one and drive a broken brown spike of glass again and again deep into my throat. Kill my brain. For once and for all stop the voices, the maddening, endless-loop, unremitting pigsnot.

In my jacket pocket, on the chair across the room, was a pint of Ralph's vodka, wrapped tightly in its brown paper bag. A short dog. Insurance. Purchased on my ride back from the movies.

Locating the jug in the dark, I cracked the seal and took a long pull. Better—immediately better. The combination of Mad Dog and vodka always works—until the next morning.

Standing naked in the half-light from the hallway, I lit a cigarette and caught my image in the bedroom window. At first, what I saw appeared distorted by the glass like a gag mirror in a funhouse. The body parts of the five-foot-seven-inch human before me appeared mismatched. Thoughtlessly assembled. The overweight, muscleless torso had short, thick arms. It topped off two hairy, log-shaped legs. The likeness reminded me of an encyclopedia sketch of a prehistoric biped, some half-monkey depicted in an early phase of evolution.

Shifting my weight to correct the resemblance, I changed positions. What I saw now wasn't funny. This was me. These odd components. This belly and the balding head and tattooed arms and these stumpy pins with the thick chest were mine. The newsroom—my brain—sent me a bulletin. It notified me that there would never come a day when the owner of this curious, runt body would enter a clothier or a sporting goods store and not have to ask for the fucking boys department.

I BEGAN TO CONSIDER what measures would be necessary for me to retrieve the taxi license. Number one: I might try telephoning the theater. But I immediately rejected this notion as preposterous. Living humans had stopped answering telephones in L.A. movie theaters years ago. All you get these days are recorded film times and nonsense announcement advertising guff. Choice two was for me to put my clothes back on and return to Santa Monica Boulevard in Hollywood, retrace my steps, talk my way past the ticket-taker at the Tiki Theater, then go inside to the back row where I had been sitting. Most likely I had lost my taxi permit there. While my cock was out and my pants were around my ankles on the theater's floor and I was ejaculating on the face and hair of the weird shim, my plastic license must have slipped from my pocket. But— if that was the case—it didn't matter anyway. Not now. The license was gone, swept up by the guy bagging the trash. So actually, in fact, there was nothing to do. Not a goddamn thing.

Fuck it!

I hated being stuck driving a cab. Since taking the gig again, my life had been drained of meaning. Stalled. The taxi business extracts the vital fluids from a man's body twelve hours a day, six days a week, a drop at a time. L.A. cab driving isn't useful work. It is human refuse relocation, the transportation of decomposing flotsam from one plastic fast-food neighborhood to the next.

Wanting to make sure I hadn't lost anything else in the theater, I searched through my keys and the other shit on the dresser.

All my stuff seemed to be there. Opening my wallet, I checked its contents also. My Social Security card and my ATM card were both there. The driver's license too. I was still drunk, but my hands were shaking, and I was unable to guide the ATM card back into its leather slot. It and my Social Security card exploded from my fingers onto the dresser. I had to settle for sweeping the items off the flat surface, then dumping them back onto the bureau.

Sitting on my bed, lighting a new cigarette, I sucked the smoke far down into my chest. Maybe the loss of the taxi license was a good thing. A sign. Fate. A wake-up call. Fuck it!

THE NEXT MORNING, I called in sick. Most of the time I slept and puked and then drank pink Pepto stomach-coater from my night table.

Sober now, I reached a hated decision: I knew that I had to go back down to the Santa Monica city hall and get a duplicate license. The new day dispatcher at L.A. Taxi, a rat-faced dwarf fuck named Percy, didn't like me and I didn't like him. If he discovered that I'd lost my permit, he would joyfully dime me out to Amir, the boss, and I would be suspended until I replaced the license. There was no way out. I would have to spend my day with a hangover, waiting again for three hours in that endless moron line and pay another fifty bucks for my carelessness of last night.

Lying there, I smoked a couple of cigarettes and took several hits from the short dog on my night table.

My last trip to the Business Permit Division of Santa Monica's municipal building had ended badly. An incident occurred between me and a subhuman fuckhole also waiting in line. The episode concluded with me attempting to murder this putz by way of stabbing him with a ballpoint pen. In the windup, the clerical guy in the gray cop uniform behind the PERMIT window came out after me. I was threatened with pepper spray, made to suffer through a wants-and-warrants check on the computer, then sent to the back of the line, where I had to complete a new four-page cabby application.

Rehashing the evil memory made my hangover worse. So bad, in fact, that my solution was to telephone the Liquor Locker on Pacific Avenue two blocks away and have Mike the day guy deliver me a fifth of Stoli. Fuck it!

HERE'S WHAT HAPPENED ON my last trip: the catastrophe started out in innocence. It was April. A normal seventy-five-degree day in L.A. The turd in front of me in the NEW APPLICATIONS/RENEWAL queue was a four-hundred-pound monster cabby piggo with glutinous, bulging eyes, wearing a filthy, ten-year-old L.A. Rams cap. To be candid, I have an unreasonable detestation of "large" humans. A psychic loathing. (Possibly some past-life, twelfth-century curse where I was chained in marriage to a hideous lardassed bitch who rarely bathed her twat.)

Any other time, I would have ignored the infected shithole ahead of me, but that morning I wasn't myself. Leaving home, an hour before, I had made the error of checking my mailbox only to discover a surprise notice of intent to audit from the Internal Revenue Service. In an effort to ease my distress, on my way to Santa Monica City Hall I got drunk on a pint of Ralph's Supermarket gin. So, by the time I arrived in the Renewal Department, I was overmedicated and clearly in no mood to be fucked with.

It was blubberass shitbreath who started the trouble and nearly got the comeuppance he deserved.

Against my will I found myself trapped in that stupid line between him and two new taxi applicants. While stuck there, I would be subjected to listening to an endless tale of outlandish, regurgitated taxi driver bullshit. An interminable, witless fabrication spontaneously invented by fatfuck pusshole to beguile and astound the new guys behind me. A moronic tale about how, at gunpoint, fatbody had been held up in his cab by a supposed crack-smoking stick-up man and his make-believe blonde-ho-bitch girlfriend. According to blimpfuck's rendering, this would-be gunman and his girlfriend had hijacked him and his taxi up over the Grapevine on Route 5 toward fucking Bakersfield. Complete unadulterated ratvomit, I promise you. Two billion percent bunk. Bogus, spurious pigsnot shitdrool.

For a long time in the hallway line I had been waiting quietly, half-whacked on my gin, reading the *New York Times Book Review* and minding my own beeswax. I had successfully managed to ignore whaleass, who stood only inches in front of me wearing Walkman earphones and lip-synching along to a Rolling Stones CD. "Pleased to meet you. Hope you guess my name . . ."

Up to this point, porkfuck had been reasonably untroublesome, wheezing gently to himself. Farting intermittently, whiling away his time by gobbling handfuls of Snickers bite-sized candy bars from the bib pocket of the largest pair of rancid Levi's overalls known to fucking Jesus.

My problem began when lardboy apparently decided that he was thirsty from the ingestion of fifty or sixty of his candy bars. Apparently, the goon required money for the soda machine because he began twisting and snorting, contorting his huge hippo ass to allow his bloated pink paw to get into the pants pockets of his contaminated overalls.

As I said before, it was a warm day. In that municipal unair-conditioned hallway it was, in fact, a baking motherfucker. So naturally, watching pussman, I was put off and irritated.

To avoid impending contamination, I was forced to reposition myself against the wall. From there I could safely witness fartman and his pocket-change-seeking gymnastics while experiencing a combination of revulsion and fascination.

Sixty seconds later, panting and struggling, acidic pellets of sweat had already formed on the brow of gordo's elephantine noggin. These drops collected quickly and began the inevitable descent to the bib of his unwashed playsuit.

At the end of this near-death effort, red-faced and neck veins pulsating, a hand successfully emerged from his pocket with two one-dollar bills. But no change. Apparently blubbershit would need to seek out financial options.

Naturally, he turned in my direction and began speaking.

At first, my disgust was so acute that I was unable to decipher his grunts. They were unrecognizable and oinklike. Garbled petitions from a mutated, steroid-bloated, slaughterhouse hogfuck.

Employing a delay tactic, to recover myself and to avoid a reply, I tried looking away and appearing preoccupied. This maneuver, of course, failed.

To my horror, garbagedump-shitmountain stepped closer. Dangerously close. Now I was able to feel the breath
from his huge hoghole, as he re-formed his request and let
it tumble from his pigsnout. "Hey, shorty," he said, gasping,
"got change for a buck?"

My reaction was physical. Completely involuntary. I stepped
back. Farther back, only to find myself experiencing the onset
of dizziness, nausea, and intestinal cramping. Naturally, for
both health and psychological reasons, it was imperative that
I continue to ignore the cocksucker.

Not so for the two new taxi applicants in the line behind
me. Luckily for me, one of them came forward and produced a
handful of silver. He exchanged these coins for the moist bills
in blimpboy's swollen fist.

Next thing I know, sweatass is oozing past me—making
physical contact—then rumbling down the corridor in the direction of the soda machine.

Now my real trouble began. In short order, my sanity would
be eviscerated, and the voices in the newsroom in my head
would begin screaming for more sedation and I, out of necessity, would need to invent a plan to murder this fetid monstros-
ity again and again. It would come down to my life or his.

When lardbuilding returned with his three Dr. Peppers, a
conversation began between him and the two dudes behind me.
It was this interaction that would ultimately rupture my sanity.

As luck would have it, these new applicants were certifiable
imbeciles, slavering born-again graduates of a state-sponsored
drug rehab lockdown in Valencia. Sixty days clean. Both richly
tattooed and on probation from years of L.A. gang violence,
street chemistry, and probable spousal battery.

So there I am, marooned between hippofat and the sober,
brain-damaged Einstein twins in an airless hallway, unable
to extricate myself from a streaming tale of contemptible
barfvomit, being tormented by listening to what the ho bitch
said to her boyfriend and then what the crackhead said back,

and what hogshit himself said after that, when she asked him if he thought she was pretty, and how the crackhead's gun was a .44 Smith and Wesson magnum like Clint Eastwood's, and how the pistol's barrel felt pressed up against his bloated temple. And on and on about powerlessness and Jesus and George Bush and lethal injection and how shitbucket himself planned to single-handedly disarm his assailant—"gun or no gun"—and how, as they sped out of the 7-11's driveway on Melrose Avenue, they nearly slammed into two pink Harley-Davidson motorcycles owned by two gay guys in leather chaps, and how the crackhead's gun misfired as they skidded past a Hollywood patrol car.

Witnessing this outrageous harangue, my stomach cramping became worse, and I began to experience respiratory impairment. I seemed to be on the verge of some sort of fit or spasm. To ward off my impending seizure, in self-defense I grasped the pen clipped to my shirt pocket—a medium-point Papermate Everflow Retractable—and prepared to defend against this assault to my sanity.

Unfortunately for me, whaleboy's cholesterol-induced recitation was far from over. His excitement had caused him to hyperventilate and turn bright pink and he appeared to be on the verge of bursting an artery or having a spontaneous ejaculation.

Barfman spewed on. At this point in his nonsense, low-rent, TV horseshit doggerel, he was on the Grapevine in a nine-car pileup, after slamming into the guardrail at a hundred and twenty miles an hour. Police cars and emergency vehicles arrived on the scene. The paramedic team announced to all present that they would have to amputate the ho-bitch's leg after the Jaws of Life had pried them all out of the wreck. Greaseman himself single-handedly disarmed his assailant by using a Vietnam kung-fu hold, and a grateful CHP officer declared that he was recommending him for a citation for heroism and good citizenship.

Finally, I could tolerate no more. Trembling, struggling to

breathe, and on the verge of a self-diagnosed petit mal convulsion, I was compelled to act.

I began yelling at the huge, bulbous atrocity. I commanded him to—if he doesn't mind too very fucking much—to just please shut the fuck up for sixty motherfucking seconds. To underscore the urgency of my request and punctuate my sincerity, I held my ballpoint pen—point unretracted—in a stabbing posture above my head, and offered to plunge it into the fat goon cocksucker's eye socket if he so much as uttered one more piglike grunt from his fucking hogfuck shithole pigsnout.

UNFORTUNATELY, NO GOOD DEED goes unpunished. As I've already said, I am no stranger to public humiliation. Moments later, the guy behind the plastic see-through renewal window began showering me with an assortment of indignities and aerosol-powered cop weapons. Additional backup was summoned, and I found myself threatened with arrest. I was even made to pass my body twice through the building's metal detector before they finally allowed me to fill out a new application.

HEARING MIKE FROM LIQUOR Locker knock on my door, I pulled myself together and slipped on my pants. The quart of Stoli came to nineteen bucks. I told Mike to add on an extra five for himself, then signed the receipt.

The Lakers game was about to start. Maybe, I thought, I'll try telemarketing again. I can't do this cab shit no more. Life's too short. Then I cracked my new jug, took a long hit, and went in to brush my teeth.

THEBOBBY

SOMETIMES THINGS JUST GO south. They spiral down into the shitter and it all happens before you know it.

I'd been evicted from my apartment in Venice and was taken in, short term, by a friend, Thebobby, an ex-New York hustler and actor-wannabe. His noisy return that afternoon woke me up.

From my bedroom—the living room couch—I could hear him in the kitchen, then outside in the backyard with Adolf and Ava, his Gestapo Dobermans, throwing a goddamn tennis ball for them against the metal garage door. The thudding and barking pissed me off and made my hangover worse.

When he was done with the dogs, he reentered the house. I guess he'd decided that I'd had enough sleep.

Thebobby is a cab driver too. We'd met at our taxi garage, A-Betta Transportation in El Segundo. After I hit bottom this last time and got my pink 3-DAY-PAY-UP-OR-QUIT notice from the landlord, it was Thebobby who offered me his couch. Like I said, short term. He'd been in L.A. for a year, and the house he bought was purchased from the money left to him by his pops in Bay Ridge. Thebobby had given up his limo job and selling street weed to move to Culver City and chase fame in L.A.

He was just back, he said, from an audition on a new fall cop show called *The Lawyers*.

His taxi was parked in the driveway and he'd stopped in for a few minutes to change clothes and play with his Dobermans.

Yanking the curtains open, he stood in front of me in sunglasses and a new vested blue suit, white shirt, and tie. He looked like a guy running for city council, or a six-foot-three live TV commercial for polyester Secret Service agents.

"Shake my hand, bro," he said. "I juss got me a callback. My first fuckin' call-back evva in L.A.!"

I shook the hand.

"You gettin' up now?"

"I am up. I was asleep until fifteen minutes ago. Now I'm up. Wide awake."

"How come ya still in bed at five in the affanoon? You waz partyin' again las' night, right?"

"Right," I said, lighting a Lucky from the pack on the coffee table. "I worked until two, then did some reading. Henry Miller. But I'm not partying now. Today happens to be my day off."

"Lez go. I'm buyin' ya dinna."

TEN MINUTES LATER MY roomie and I were in his cab on our way to Hu's Chinese in West L.A. Szechuan food. Out of necessity, en route, I requested a stop at Ralph's Supermarket's liquor department for a pint of 80-proof to rid my body of its shakes.

Hu's is always crowded at dinnertime and there is usually a line outside. But we got lucky. Thebobby is pushy and has a football player's thick neck, and using an excuse, he squeezed past the dozen or so citizen mooches waiting in line by the front door. I followed.

Once inside, he spotted two college-age girls about to leave, paying the waiter at their table. My roommate is also pretty, and the sight of him weaving his way toward them caught their eye. They smiled obligingly, then took extra time settling their bill, long enough for Thebobby to glom the table for us and edge out the chumps waiting in line.

ME

[*Now seated, I arrange a new setting of silverware on my napkin and notice shitlooking water spots on one of the utensils—I wipe the stains off and ignore the menu*] I'm having the Kung Pao shrimp . . . What're you having?

THEBOBBY

[*Glances at the order sheet, then tosses it down*] You always have the shrimp, man. Ga-head, I'm payin', take the fuckin' plunge, get somethin' good. Somethin' different. I dare ya.

ME

May I have your permission to order whatever the fuck it is I want? For your information, I have the shrimp primarily because I like it. I'm a Kung Pao shrimp kinda guy.

THEBOBBY

[*Removes his sunglasses*] I ain' tha hungry. The shrimp's cool, I guess. Kung Pao is cool. [*Gets up from the table*] You want water?

ME

Sure. Okay—but you know—half a glass—with lemon.

THEBOBBY

I remember about the lemon. We've discussed the goddamn lemon sixteen thousand times.

[*I watch as the tall would-be actor walks to the back of the dining room area to a self-service counter. He adds ice to two glasses and from a pitcher, fills them halfway. He adds slices of lemon. During the interval, the waiter arrives at our table with a note pad. I give him the oder. By the time Thebobby returns, the waiter has gone]*

THEBOBBY

Here, water with lemon. Lemon water. [*He hands me my glass*]

ME

[*Holding it up to the light, I examine it for signs of Chinese restaurant bacteria*] Yessir. Thank you. [*I fill our glasses the rest of the way up from the pint bottle in my jacket pocket*]

THEBOBBY

[*Watches me pour the whiskey*] You're a juicer, bro. A stone juicer.

ME

I drink, Bob. It's the no-shit truth.

THEBOBBY

Man, I hope I get that cop-show gig. So much fuckin' betta than sweating my ass on the seat of a taxi in L.A. traffic ten hours a day, six days a week. [*He raises his glass*] Well, mazel tov, or whateva the fuck they say. Ya know—good luck. [*He takes a hit.*] Ah-sa-lu-ta.

ME

Ditto. [*I clink our glasses*] First today—from a glass. [*Pounding my drink, I pour myself another*]

THEBOBBY

Hey, what about the writing? You tell me you're a fuckin' writer but I never seen nothin' you wrote. Hey, how 'bout this: you write a screenplay and put me in it.

ME

I'm not writing much these days. I'm on hiatus.

THEBOBBY

Well, when you do put somethin' good togetha, remember me. I'm your man. We'll be partners.

ME

You're paying for dinner. I guess you must've had a good night yesterday.

THEBOBBY

I made a damn decent hit. No shit. Sun Tzu, the dude who wrote *The Art of War* a thousand years ago, says, "Seize the day."

ME

Sun Tzu never said "Seize the day." *Carpe diem* is a Latin phrase. Sun Tzu was a maniacal, self-obsessed putz.

THEBOBBY

Whatevah.

ME

Anyway, thanks for the food. And congratulations.

THEBOBBY

I got lucky. Well—not really lucky. "A man makes his own luck," my father, Paolo Anthony Di Vencenzo, used to say. Pop was no relation to Sun-fuckin'-Tzu.

ME

Point taken.

THEBOBBY

[*Finishes his drink and pours a fresh one*] Okay, well . . . Wait!
Okay, I'll tell you about it. Lemme start from the beginning.
{*Takes a long hit.*] See, there's this old guy, Alvin—the girls at
the club call him Ancient Alvin.

ME

Sounds like a big tipper. Where do I meet him?

THEBOBBY

Can I just tell it? Wanna just clamp it for four seconds, okay?

ME

Sure. You're my host. You're buying.

THEBOBBY

Well, Ancient Alvin is drunk as a snake and he's standing
on Olympic, outside Strip Euphoria—about three-thirty
last night. You know I been hangin' there in my spare time.
Tiffany dances there.

ME

Tiffany's the short one, right?

THEBOBBY

No, bro. Thaz Debbie. Debbie's the short one. Huge gazoonga
titties. Tiff 's the tall one. Anyway, just let me tell it, okay?

ME

Okay. But I met a black lap dancer that time and an Asian
girl—which one's Tiffany?

THEBOBBY

[*Drains his glass*] I ain' talkin' 'bout that black blowjob bitch or Debbie or that greedy Sri Lankan kooze, Vikki. Like I said, Tiffie's tall. I don't know why I wasted my fucking time with that fuckin' Vikki. Ask me, Vikki belongs in a squirrel box. But—now that you bring it up—fuckin' Vikki is a major part of the problem that—bottom line—could have degenerated into a full-on impervious shitstorm . . . But no, this is Tiffany. You know, blonde. About five-ten. Nice non-plastic juggernauts. Full, natural C-cup.

ME

Okay. No silicone implants. Okay. Back to Ancient Alvin. Kindly do not digress.

THEBOBBY

Have you heard of that women's deal, La Leche? I'd like to join that deal . . . Then I found out they don't let guys in.

ME

[*Polishing my knife*] I never met Tiffany. I'm pretty sure I never met her.

THEBOBBY

Yeah you did. She's pretty. Real friendly. Okay, now I remember! You're right. You didn't meet her at the club that time. You saw us together a couple of Sundays ago. We were at the Beverly Center. Her brother's the attorney guy who used to handle one of the Beatles—Ringo, I think. You know, Tiff-an-eee. I been doing her pretty steady. [*He rubs his crotch*] She loves watching Shaq go to the hoop. A tonsillectomy specialist. [*Standing up, he mimes holding a woman's head in the act of giving a blowjob*] I like watching her face while she gulps down the love juice.

ME

Bob, a tonsillectomy is a surgical procedure.

THEBOBBY

I like when you correct me alla time. Fuck you very much.

ME

Right. So . . .

THEBOBBY

I'm telling you what happened, goddamnit! Anyway, she's been workin' at Strip Euphoria less than two months. She was the bartender at Tigress before that. Out by the airport. Before that she was dancing downtown . . . The first night I met her—I'm having a lousy night in my cab, right, so I decide to knock off early and stop into the club for a drink to cheer myself up. One drink, right? There's no cover on Tuesday nights and G & T's are two-for-five. Anyway, I park my cab around the corner on Sawtelle and go inside and there she is, on stage. Like I said, Tiff is tall.

ME

I remember now. The blonde. Right?

THEBOBBY

I like 'em tall. With long legs. Bottom line, that's my thing. I'm definitely a leg man. Leg and ass.

ME

[*I pour myself a fresh drink*] Right.

THEBOBBY

So, when her set is over, I can't help it—I'm done, right? Completely in-fuckin'-love. I gotta have this bitch or die. So, I follow her into the ladies' crapper. Eddy, the bouncer guy, he's busy with some asshole arguing about a credit card—doing his job—throwing the guy out—so, any-who, I follow Tiff right into the ladies crappah, ya know. And while she's taking a snake's hiss, I stand up over the stall next to hers and ask her for her phone number, you know.

ME

Love at first sight.

THEBOBBY

Hey man, the kooz dig it. [*He gestures*] You gotta have basketballs. Bottom line, dancers are totally into that kinda demonstratively aggressive shit. So, I pass her this roll of toilet papah—ya know—over the top of the stall, big smile on my face—and I say, "Need any help?"

ME

You were going to tell me about Alvin.

THEBOBBY

Okay, right! Fuck! Okay, so—like I say—I'm outside Strip Euphoria parked down the block a few doors from the entrance. I'm havin' a lousy night, right. Bottom line, I've done two airports since six fuckin' p.m.

ME

[*Our Kung Pao chicken arrives, and the guy places the dishes and a large bowl of rice before us, then walks off. Presently, I detect what appears to be an alien strand of hair floating in my peanut sauce.*]

From the texture and length, I deduce that this hair is Asian and from someone's nose. Using the end prong of my fork, I move the disgusting-looking fucker to the side of my plate] Just tell it, okay? And please omit the term "bottom line."

THEBOBBY

Right. Okay.

ME

And would you mind leaving out all asides pertaining to vaginal secretions and extraneous minutiae?

THEBOBBY

Hey bro, it's background. You're the writer. This is background for your screenplay.

ME

I don't write screenplays. And if I ever begin to write one, kindly shoot me in the head. Might we press on?

THEBOBBY

[*Begins to eat*] So, bottom line, here I am—waiting, filling out my trip form, and hangin' in front of the club. Okay? No Ancient Alvin so far, okay?

ME

[*I finish my drink and tentatively continue to eat my Kung Pao while scanning my plate for foreign matter*] Okay.

THEBOBBY

Then I hear this noise and look up and there he is, Ancient-fucking-Alvin, standing there asserting his need to get into my fuckin' taxicab. I mean this dude is maybe seventy-five

years old and ripped out of his Versaces. I got no idea who the
fuckah is. He ain't shit to me, right? I know nothing, right?

ME

Right.

THEBOBBY

So, ya know, I'm like all—who the fuck are you? You're way
too fuckin' juiced to get into my taxi. Right?

ME

So, you said.

THEBOBBY

So, I'm like—yo pops, get the fuck away from my cab. Right?

ME

Enter Ancient Alvin. Intoxicated. Drunk as a snake.

THEBOBBY

Not so fast. I'm getting to that part . . . Anyway, he's totally weaving. Like I say, fuckin' blotto. Yelling "Open the door.
Open the goddamn door!"

ME

You paint a clear picture. Bottom line.

THEBOBBY

So now he's saying shit about how he called a taxi twenty minutes ago. [*Begins eating his Kung Pao, but sets his fork down after
two bites and pours himself another boost*]

ME

So, you popped the door locks and let him into the car. You made lemonade out of lemons and Alvin gave you a big tip.

THEBOBBY

I fuckin' wish! Now, whoa, out of the club comes Vikki, the Sri Lankan douchebag I have previously mentioned—I'll get my PB on this. I promise ya that—Vikki personally is a complete one hundred percent selfish twat. Vikki person-ally—bottom line—would pick the corn out of your shit and resell it to Ralph's-fucking-Supermarket. Anyway, next second, she's standing there making out with old Moses. You know, leaning on my taxi. Sucking his tongue an' shit. Right thah.

ME

Okay.

THEBOBBY

Fuckin' disgusting. Of course, I am obliged to be a witness to this uninspiring, cock-teasing interlude of spit exchange. I'm watchin' this, right? Him rubbin' her fake titties an' all. The whole thing. Then, believe this, he stuffs two hundreds down her top. Two hundreds! Okay? Not twenties or fifties. I see it all . . . The dude's roll is totally Franklins and Grants.

ME

Ah, Alvin the Rich.

THEBOBBY

So, I mean, what am I gonna do? I'm screwed city here, right? But now I see there just might be a few bucks in it for moi. You know, so, very fuckin' reluctantly, I press my button and Miss

Evil Tarantula-ass pops her head inside and says: "Hi, Bobby
sweetie"—like we're supposed to be old grade school classmates
or some shit because I let her gargle my Shaq one night a while
back—"This is Alvin," she says. "A dear personal acquaintance.
Alvin is going to Marina del Rey." She whispers, intimate-like,
"Odette's place."

ME

Odette?

THEBOBBY

Odette runs hookers at the Marina Club Apartments. Vikki
knows that I know about Odette because Odette is actually
the code name of this rich twat who runs the bitches—they
all call her Odette, okay? The girls from Strip Euphoria bring
their johns to Odette's or refer them there. I have personally transported many fares to Odette's and Vikki, of course,
knows this fact.

ME

Could there possibly be an end in sight to this meandering,
uninspiring tale of class struggle and capitalist exploitation?

THEBOBBY

You bet your ass. Believe it, there's a fuckin' end! You'd better
believe there's a fuckin' end.

ME

Okay, so . . .

THEBOBBY

Anyway, this deceitful Sri Lankan douchebag non-fuckin'-
amigo of mine Vikki, in order to rid herself of her problem,

places the disgusting prince of puke, evil Rasputin hizzself—
in my cab. Okay? And the very second he's on the seat and
she slams the door closed, I know I'm had. Ancient Al is a
class-A major ball-breaker. You know, complete total attitude . . . I mean, you gotta understand something—now it's
almost four o'clock—I was inside before drinkin' G & T's at
the bar for a couple hours—chatting up the snatch. Tiff don't
care. She's open-minded. She's been free-pouring me the shit
every time I turn around. Talking sweet an' all. Tapping her
knuckles on the bar every time she serves me a blast. Totally
coverin' my action. Nice girl, Tiff. You remember, like I said,
full natural C-cup. But still, I mean, I ain' put no dollars on
the fuckin' meter. And I'm aware of this, believe me! In fact,
I'm obsessing on my personal cab-driver financial inadequa-
cies. You know, like mental neurosis is doggin' my shit . . . but
now here's Ancient-fucking-Alvin wanting a ride to Odette's.
See what I'm sayin'?

ME

[*I finish my food*] Okay, let's have it. The point, please. The bottom line.

THEBOBBY

Right. I know. It gets worse. Anyway, deranged Alvin the
hard-on, like I've already said, is totally buzzed. And now I'm
supposed to deliver this subhuman, quarrelsome cocksucker
to Odette's? I mean—I'm all—I don't think so. How would that
look? I mean, I know Odette. Odette is my friend, right? Odette
has done me one or two solids over the last several months.
Correct or incorrect?

ME

Ah—now I understand the dilemma—Alvin's got a pocket full
of money.

THEBOBBY

Therein lies my fuckin' quandary. See? So, anyway, as we begin the ride, Ancient Alvin is now totally yanking my Shaq—dissin' everything in sight. Telling me how dirty my cab is, how to drive: Stop here, pull over, get me a pack of Camel Filters. You know, that shit . . . But fortunately for yours truly, the prick has thrown a Jefferson on the front seat, which, of course, to a great extent, reverse-exacerbates the situation and, in a manner of speaking, counter-fuckin-balances my excess pain and suffering in having to transport his lame, mean geriatric ass.

ME

Right. A Jefferson on the front seat. I'm with you.

THEBOBBY

Yeah, but, like I said, it gets worse.

ME

Okay, so . . .

THEBOBBY

Anyway, after dissin' my shit for five minutes, he starts in about what a champion wandsman he is and how much he spent on that bitch Vikki to lap-dance on his teeny Herman all night. Like, what else is new, right? But—and here's the crux of the deal—I can now totally peep from his conduct that if I drop the drunken fuck at Odette's, I am, in fact, violating my special business arrangement with her. No matter how much money the ancient doofus has stashed in his Calvins. Right? I mean, in no way can me bringing trouble into Odette's place be interpreted as a positive career move. And, of course, that leads me back to the scheming Sri Lankan silicone douchebag from hell, Vikki, who has contributed greatly to all the fuckin' consternation to begin with. Now you see my point?

ME

[*Stacking the salt and pepper shakers and my glass in a pyramid*] I'm not sure. But I'm not sure it matters. I do know that you've been at the bar all night getting free pours from Tiffany with the full C-cup, putting moves on whatever mostly naked female wanders by, following the lap dancers into the john, et cetera. And now you're back in the cab trying to earn a living. And you meet Alvin, who you do not want to take to Odette's palace. Have I got it all?

THEBOBBY

[*Knocks over my pyramid*] Yeah, that's pretty much it. Bottom line.

ME

I like the food here. Thanks for dinner.

THEBOBBY

And I like herpes.

ME

Can we go?

THEBOBBY

[*Motions for me to pass him the bottle, then pours himself another fresh drink*] How 'bout another glass of Drano? I'll be done tellin' ya in two minutes.

ME

[*I push my glass across the table so Thebobby can pour*] Continue, please. You talked me into it.

THEBOBBY

[*Allowing me the last drink in the bottle*] Okay, so now, anyway, I figure, what are my options here? I mean, the dude's in the fucking cab, right? I've got no choice but to drop dick-knob at Odette's. Trouble or no trouble. I mean, if Odette's gonna get mad, she's gonna get mad, right? Vikki is the source of the fucking shit and consternation, not me. I'm totally William Jefferson Clinton here, right?

ME

Just finish the story.

THEBOBBY

Okay, so anyway, we're in the cab and I'm driving. I'm resigned to my fate, see? I head south on Sawtelle toward the entrance to the 405. I've made my right, off Olympic and start catching all the lights, just as Alvin-the-Hideous begins to ralph his cookies . . .

ME

Jesus!

THEBOBBY

Exactly. [*Smells his hands as if to remember*] We're talking full-on Stephen-fuckin'-King here. It took me twenty minutes to clean the funk out of the car and most of a bottle of that spray shit that they sell at the 7-11. Anyway, after he starts spewing, as one might presume, my immediate concern shifts to self-fucking-preservation. I hit the brakes, stop the cab, jump out, and hustle around to the back door. It pops open just in time for Ancient Al to tumble his bony rectum ass from the cab and gash his noggin on the asphalt. Believe that shit?

ME

Enthralling. No other word for it.

THEBOBBY

I ain't fuckin' yankin' ya dick here. This is the straight shit. But there's no time to say a novena for the ninety-year-old cocksucker because, stellar fucking professional juicehead that he is, Ancient Al arises from the pavement relatively un-damaged—that is, except for the blood an' shit—making some comment like, "Oops, I musta slipped." But then, just as I get the old guy up on his pins, I discover that he has yet to end his demonstration on the finer technical merits of projectile puk-ing—except now, it's on the trunk of my cab. Taxi number 371. My steady car. Ya dig?

ME

I'm starting to enjoy this. Blood, betrayal, silicone implants, hundred-dollar bills. It has everything.

THEBOBBY

So, anyway, I get him up and back into the cab, then wheel over to the Texaco on Pico Boulevard—all this through con-secutive fucking dry heave- and upchucking-spasms, mind you. Once at the Tex, Alvin appears to have finished ral-phing, so I pull him out and muscle his now dead-to-the-world-and-bleeding old asshole up into the front seat, where he won't be the source of additional mayhem. Whereas I should, by rights, have left the cazzo doofus facedown at the curb as soon as he started making trouble. But something is telling me to be mindful of the guy's well-being. A little voice, you know?

ME

That little voice perhaps emanating from the roll of fifties and hundreds residing in Ancient Alvin's khakis.

THEBOBBY

Hey, pal, you know, "You cast your bread upon the waters."

ME

Sun Tzu. *The Art of War.*

THEBOBBY

Blow me, okay? Anyway, I hose out the cab as best I can and wipe it down with paper towels.

ME

If you'll notice, the bottle is done. Can we—may we—just cut to the fucking chase?

THEBOBBY

We're there. This is the chase. Now it gets good.

ME

So, Alvin's in the front seat, the meter's running, and at least you're putting money on your trip sheet. And, as you've said, you hosed out the puke. What now?

THEBOBBY

[*Takes the last hit from his glass*] You wouldn't believe my fucking goddamn day. So, what's a responsible-citizen cab driver to do?

ME

I don't know, Bobby. Find out where the man lives and make sure he gets home. Just a guess.

THEBOBBY

[*Removes a wad of bills from his pocket and fans them out face-down on the table*] And what do you think I discover lying on the front seat of taxi number 371—beneath Ancient Alvin's wrinkly ass butt? Fourteen hundred American dollars.

ME

[*Seriously disgusted*] You took Alvin's money? Swell, Bobby. You rolled a feeble, helpless juicer. Well done.

THEBOBBY

[*Pushes the money across to my side of the table*] Hey, bro, wake up. This could have fallen out of his pants anywhere. In the shitter at the club, in the elevator at his apartment building. Anywhere. Fucking Vikki could have mugged him for it if she had the intelligence of a gerbil. It just so happens it was in plain sight on the seat of taxi number 371.

ME

I see. Right there on the seat. Not in his pants pocket or his wallet. How fortuitous. Then what happened?

THEBOBBY

Ye of no fuckin' faith. Well, naturally I deposited him on the front steps at Odette's. Safe and sound and out of harm's way. Comatose, naturally. In Six Flags–fuckin'–dreamland. Ask me, it's better than the chump deserved.

ME

[*I shove the money back across the table*] I think I'd like to pay for my own dinner tonight. [*I reach into my pocket for my wallet*]

THEBOBBY

Hey, bro, bottom line, life is improvisation. Opportunity meeting necessity. "Seize the day."

ME

Thanks, Mother Teresa. I pass. You're a user. A class-A asshole. A consummate prick.

THEBOBBY

[*Disgusted*] Hey, bro, I catch a break and slide into a couple of bucks the hard way—upside down—with a fucking juice-mooch puking all over me and my cab, and suddenly you're the moral fucking fiber of the taxi industry. Dude, wake up and smell the cat shit.

ME

You mean Doberman shit, don't you?

THEBOBBY

So what! There's a whole bank account more where that came from. Alvin's rich as Fort-friggin'-Knox, for chrissakes. He's retired from the diamond business or some goddamn thing. Vikki told me—not that I believe anything that kooze-bitch says.

ME

You dumped him out on the street without any money. You rolled the man.

THEBOBBY

Hey, bro, let's not make me out the bad guy here, okay?

ME

Bottom line, it stinks, Bob. It stinks like shit.

THEBOBBY

Lemme ask you something, Cardinal Mahoney: after you got evicted for being a non-payee, fall-down juicehead and a stiff, where you left your apartment owing your landlord over a thousand dollars in back rent, cheating him out of his hard-earned money, who gave you a couch to sleep on?

ME

You did.

THEBOBBY

Case fuckin' closed. Have I called you any names?

ME

I just realized something, Bob. Something I guess I didn't know.

THEBOBBY

Cool. What is it? I'm like all donkey ears over here.

ME

[*I get up from the table*] You're a cocksucker. Low-life scum. A punk.

THEBOBBY

[*He also stands—now smiling*] Okay, so who's paying for your dinner, mister purer than virgin menstrual piss? Me or you?

ME

You are, prick . . . You're the man with the fourteen hundred in his pocket. But if you don't mind, can we stop back by the market on the way home? I find that I'm running a quart low. Would that be too much to ask?

THEBOBBY

Sure. You know me. Anything for a pal.

1647 Ocean Front Walk

NOTHING STOPS IT—the emptiness of being alone.

It was September. Still morning rush hour, and I was chugging along Ocean Avenue in Santa Monica, empty. Another cloudless, flawless fucking L.A. day.

My Chevy taxi #855 had been overheating consistently for a week in the summer heat, and for the last two shifts in a row the problem was worse. My cab was an ex-Highway Patrol cruiser with over 200,000 miles on the odometer.

I hated being assigned to this vehicle. Not only because of its cop history, but because of the steady night guy who drove #855: a fat Guatemalan fuck named Sergio. Sergio refused to report mechanical problems on the car the way it says to do on the SHIFT TURN-IN form, which everybody is required to sign. According to a rumor passed along by JJ, the mechanic, my night man Sergio was devoting the bulk of his evenings to smoking cheap reefer and chasing crackhead pussy downtown near the Staples Center. The asshole was apparently unconcerned by the steam hissing out from under the hood of cab #855. That left me—on my shift time—to deal with all the repair stuff. I'd complained repeatedly, without result. This was because, coincidentally, Raoul the night dispatcher was Sergio's brother-in-law, his sidekick at hounding pussy and, not coincidentally, also a prize Guatemalan sack of shit. It had taken two hours that morning for JJ to mickey-rig #855 so I could work my shift.

While waiting in the repair shop, I'd occupied my time visualizing Sergio and Raoul frolicking in unprotected anal sex with the toothless rockhead bitches who hang out at the 9th Street off-ramp from the Harbor Freeway.

DRIVING A CAB HAD saved my sanity. For months my mind had been scalded by depression and sleeplessness. And terrible enforced solitude. I'd wake up—or come to—five or six times a night, in a rage, the faces of those I hated strangling my thoughts.

I'd diagnosed myself as too fucked up to write and made the decision to give it up completely except for the poetry I jotted down while in my cab. Everything else that I'd put on paper—each new attempt at a novel or short story—was a lie. False. Unredeemable pigshit. Hacking twelve to fifteen hours a day was all that was keeping me alive. That and Shenley's Reserve whiskey.

My oceanfront apartment was a hand-me-down from my father's cousin Paul. Three rooms facing the water in a hundred-year-old falling-down Santa Monica brick bunker, with terrible plumbing. I got the place the week before I'd started the taxi job. Uncle Paul had lived there for forty-two years under city rent control. Before he kicked off, as he was being forced into a board and care by his kids, the apartment was offered to me. Two-ninety-seven a month, in a neighborhood where three rooms went for four times that much. So, what if the tub was in the kitchen and the john had a pull chain? The place was a steal.

My second week in the apartment—swamped by half-assed home-improvement notions—I'd made the mistake of stripping the plaster from the walls that faced the exterior, baring the brick. My idea had been to seal the cracks, then cover the surface with clear lacquer. But that never happened. I began driving a taxi full time instead. Now the rubble and shit from the walls was on my floor. The best I could do was to shovel and sweep this debris into one room—the bedroom—where it was piled up waist high. I took up residence in the kitchen and pantry. My roommates were Uncle Paul's bad-tempered ghost and my deteriorated sanity.

IT HAD BEEN A week since I'd received a decent 10-21 radio call from the Sorrento Terrace on Ocean Avenue, so I decided to cruise by and see what was up. A week of not getting a call or a good fare from Marco, the day doorman, was unusual. He had my home phone number and habitually steered business my way. I'd made it a point to always tip the guy well, and I depended on one hand washing the other. The Sorrento is a swank, Spanish-style, thirty-story condo overlooking Santa Monica Bay. Many of the people living in the building are old nondrivers who use taxis to go everywhere. If you're a cabbie and have the right relationship with Marco, the place can pay off like a lotto ticket.

Turning in under the Sorrento's entrance alcove, seeing no cabs in the hold line, I was able to pull up near the front door. I caught Marco's eye, and he saluted hello, then left his post at the door to walk over to my taxi.

Leaning in my driver's window, he whispered, "Bad timing, bro."

"Why? What's up?" I said.

He wasn't smiling. "You won't like what's coming down in the elevator, but there's nothin' I can do. Party of three to Cedars-Sinai Medical Center."

"Sounds okay," I said back. "Cedars is a decent hit from here."

"It's Missus Randolph. She's the problem. She's fuckin' whacked. Her mom is the rich lady in 3019. Missus Carter. You remember. You rode her before. Nice old gal. Says 'If you would be so kind' and 'If it wouldn't be too much trouble,' all the time. Real proper."

"Sure, I know her. She walks with a walker. An exceptional person, actually. Sharp and funny. She always wants me to help her walk to the door."

"That's Gramma. So last week the old gal got diagnosed with cancer in the pancreas, and now her daughter, Missus Randolph, has totally lost her shit. Cryin' on the phone. Crazy. The cleaning crew's been up there twice already today sweeping up broken glass. You're riding Randolph, her daughter Sydney, and the lawyer guy to the ICU to visit Gramma. It won't be fun."

"Work's work," I said.

Marco leaned in close. "You look like shit. You been burning the candle at both ends?"

"No candle. Just burning."

"Listen," he whispered, "they're not down yet. Go ahead, take off. They'll ruin your day. Let this one pass. Lemme call another cab."

"No," I said, "I'm here. I got a late start today. I need the work."

"Okay. But remember—don't blame me."

Five minutes later, I was heading east on Wilshire Boulevard with Feldman the attorney in the front seat by me and Missus Randolph and her daughter, Sydney, in the back, on our way to Cedars-Sinai in Hollywood.

The striking thing about the two women in the rear of my cab was their physical similarity. Missus Randolph and her daughter might easily have been sisters. Both women were natural beauties. The girl was unusually striking, quiet and soft-spoken, in her early twenties, with the look of a young Grace Kelly. The generation difference between them didn't show.

But Marco was right. Randolph was nuts. Lady-fuckin'-Macbeth. The news of her mother's diagnosis had rendered her inconsolable. Through my rearview mirror, I watched her holding her daughter's face between her hands, crying out: "Jesus, Lord, do you hear me? I can't go on! I can't go on!" Sydney tried to contain her mom, but it was easy to see that she had her hands full. To me, Randolph's reaction seemed excessive. Grandma Carter wasn't dead yet. She had only just been diagnosed. Things change. She might get better.

While Missus Randolph continued acting up, Attorney Feldman was exhibiting the empathy and kindness of an insurance adjuster. He sat next to me, guarding his briefcase. Uninvolved, a coroner observing his colleagues sawing open a skull.

The real trouble started when we got to Beverly Hills. I'd begun to hear my cab's radiator hissing again. At Feldman's request, the A/C had been running in the stop-and-go traffic on Wilshire, and now the temperature gauge was well into the red zone.

In an effort to cool the car down, I shut off the air conditioner, then asked my passengers to open their windows. Feldman, in his blue suit, began making comments about inconvenience and grading the appearance of the cab. He wanted me to be aware that he based his tipping practices on the quality of the service provided. Attorney Feldman was a fuck and an asshole. I ignored him.

At each intersection where I caught a red light, I'd pop my gearshift into N and keep my foot on the gas pedal, revving the engine. It helped bring the blinking temperature needle back down from HOT.

As we crossed Beverly Drive and the traffic opened up, Missus Randolph began to moan. A sort of wounded animal sound. It increased steadily until it became a scream. Then she started to throw herself against the passenger door. It popped open suddenly and in terror Sydney began yelling "Pull over! Pull over!"

Hitting my brakes, I made a quick right turn onto a neighborhood side street. Shy Sydney took a full minute to wrestle her mom's grip from the door handle.

Between Randolph, my hangover, and my taxi's boiling radiator, the situation was nuts. I refused to go on and I told

Sydney and Attorney Feldman that as far as I was concerned, Randolph was unsafe to travel.

While I waited in my cab, the kid tried to pull things to-gether. She began walking her mom on the manicured grass by the sidewalk, holding her up. Feldman was out of the car too. Observing but not helping. Grudgingly, the jerk paced the women from behind.

It was useless. Randolph was too far gone. Every few steps she would go limp, then allow her body to collapse.

It was getting hot in Beverly Hills. Maybe ninety degrees. Two well-dressed pedestrians walking by, seeing Missus Ran-dolph clutching Sydney, then sprawling herself on a lawn, stopped to offer their help. Missus Randolph must finally have realized she was attracting negative attention because she started to cooperate and made an attempt to collect herself.

Twenty feet away, while watching this scene, I had my own mechanical problems. I located a two-gallon plastic coolant jug that JJ the mechanic had filled with water for me that morning, "just in case." After emptying it into the car's reser-voir, I continued racing the motor until the fucker finally be-gan to cool down.

By the time the crazy lady was ready to go on, my cab's tem-perature gauge was back down from HOT and the car was okay to drive.

BACK UNDER WAY AGAIN, when I turned onto Wilshire Bou-levard, the traffic was bumper to bumper. Feldman, fanning himself with a newspaper, had removed his suit coat and was now making a pissy face as if to imply that he regarded all Beverly Hills congestion as my responsibility.

My attention was on traffic and my cab's temperature gauge and I failed to notice that Missus Randolph was leaning for-ward, directly against my seat back. Suddenly, without a word, her arms were around my neck in an unintended choke hold.

"Help me!" she howled. "Can't you help me?"

"Christfuck!" I yelled, fighting her with one arm while jerking the steering wheel to steady the car. "Let go, goddamnit!"

Together Sydney and Feldman managed to pull her off. "This can't be happening!" she moaned. "I won't live without Mom! . . . Lord God Jesus, take me! Take me, too!"

I slammed on my brakes and pulled the cab to the curb.

Now I was totally tweaked. I began ranting, demanding that Missus Randolph calm down and shut the fuck up.

My mood and my cursing must have scared her because she instantly calmed down. Shell-shocked. Finally, she threw herself on to her daughter's lap and began weeping quietly.

Coming around to the rear passenger door, I popped it open. Me and Randolph were face-to-face.

"Hey, look," I said, leaning in, dripping with sweat, "I'm sorry I yelled at you. I know you're upset, okay? I understand what you're going through. But you almost got us clobbered by a bus. You've got to pull yourself together."

She was out of the cab and standing in front of me, propped against my taxi's rear fender, this beautiful madwoman, her green eyes blazing in the September heat.

I was startled and off-balance when she grabbed me in a desperate hug, her arms around my neck. I could feel the thinness of her cotton dress allowing her body in against mine.

Confused, I tried backing away. The sensation was strange. Sexual. Missus Randolph wouldn't let go. As she held me, I began to sense an involuntary reaction from my cock. Finally, I stepped back and forced her arms down to her sides.

"You know, don't you?" she whispered into my shirt. "You know what this's like?"

"Yes, I guess I do." I said. Then I added, "I went through it with my father."

There was a faint smile. "Mom is an amazing woman," she whispered. "I wish you could have known her."

"I do know her. She's a good, generous person."

"How do you know my mother?"

"She's been in my cab before. Several times. We've talked. I like her."

Randolph was pressing herself against me again, breathing in spasms. She began running her hands up and down my arms. "Will you hold me?"

"Sure," I said, hugging back, now aware that my cock had become fully hard.

"Can you help me?" she whispered.

"No. I don't think so."

"You have kind eyes. Tell me your name. What's your name?"

"Bruno," I said. "It's Bruno."

"My name is Claire, Bruno."

"Hello, Claire."

"I don't know what to do. Tell me what I have to do now."

The smell of her, the heat, the unreasonableness of this sudden starved intimacy had me. Again I tried to pull away, but she held herself to me.

"There's nothing to do," I said finally. "Can't you just go to the hospital and be with your mom? That's really all she needs."

The words seemed to soothe her. Claire relaxed a bit, but continued to keep her body against mine. "Mom used to be a teacher. A professor," she said. "Did you know that, Bruno?"

"No," I said. "But I'm not surprised."

Now she was holding my face in her hands, meeting my eyes. "My mother has cancer, Bruno. Fucking pancreatic cancer. She's going to die."

"You don't know that for sure."

"Oh, yes, I do. I know it. Hold me, Bruno. Please." Claire slid her arms around me again and I could feel it as she deliberately maneuvered her crotch against mine.

"We all go through this," I said into her hair. "You'll be okay."

"No. Not without Mom. I don't care anymore. I just don't care. You understand. I know that you know what I'm saying."

"Yeah," I said, "I know. I feel that way a lot."

BY THE TIME WE arrived at Cedars-Sinai, Claire's intensity was more controlled, but her mood had affected Sydney. All morning the girl had been trying to comfort her mom but now the strain of the emotional marathon had taken its toll. She was nuts too.

Both women got out immediately and rushed inside, then Feldman made his way around to my driver's window and leaned in. The meter read $28.75. He stuffed two twenty-dollar bills in my hand.

Now the jerk's attitude had changed. He faked being solicitous. "Look, my friend, my apologies for all this," he said. "Can you wait for me? For us? They may or may not be going back to Santa Monica, but I've got to be at my office for a one o'clock meeting."

He was patting his briefcase. "I have one document that requires a signature, then I'll be right back. Hopefully, barring additional hysteria, I'll be in the hospital a maximum of fifteen minutes."

MY THOUGHTS HAD BEEN on Claire and our unexpected connection. But now she was gone. Fuck Feldman, the unfeeling ghoul. "Hey," I said. I counted out his change then handed it back. "You paid me. That's that."

He handed me another twenty. Then another. "Work with me. I need your help. Candidly, I'm less enchanted with this situation than you are. I can well appreciate your hesitation."

I thought for a second, then changed my mind. I'd take his money. There was still an off chance I might see Claire again. "Okay," I said, "what the hell. I'll wait."

In the Cedars parking building it took a few minutes, but I found a space where I could keep my eye on the hospital's main entrance.

Opening my trunk, I retrieved the two-gallon plastic coolant jug I'd used earlier. I was able to talk the attendant guy into unlocking a maintenance closet for me so I could refill the container from the sink.

After I added more water to the radiator, I continued racing the motor until the car cooled off. That done, I again filled the jug from the janitor's closet. Then I turned the motor off and waited.

Alone, smoking, trying to read my *New York Times Book Review*, thoughts of Claire swarmed me. The way she pressed herself against me. The uncertainty and need and fever in her eyes. It had been months since I'd felt a woman, felt anything except my own rage and despair. Impossibly, I realized that I was in love.

No other cars were near me in the parking structure, so I unzipped my pants, then covered my cock with the newspaper and began jerking off. When I was ready to cum, I peeled off a section of paper towel from a roll I kept under the seat and blasted my load into it.

HALF AN HOUR LATER, Feldman came out the front door. Alone.

The traffic going back to the West Side was better than it had been on our way to Hollywood. Feldman wanted me to turn the A/C on again. I tried running it but gave up when the temperature gauge started climbing. After that, neither of us spoke.

His black BMW was parked in VISITOR PARKING at the Sorrento Terrace, so I pulled into the hold lot instead of dropping him at the main entrance.

He paid me, then got out. Reaching back inside the cab, he began dragging his briefcase out across the seat. "I need to ask you a question," I said.

"Make it quick. I'm in a hurry."

"About Missus Randolph."

"Christ. What is it? Speaking frankly, I've had enough of that unstable bitch for one day. I regard this entire adventure as patently ridiculous."

"Is someone picking them up? Her and Sydney? Do you think I should go back to the hospital and let them know I'm waiting?"

"Don't waste your time. Missus Randolph has clearly demonstrated her immunity to reason. From what she said, they'll be there all day. Until they're escorted out."

Now Attorney Feldman was patting his briefcase. "With the paper her mother just signed, Claire Randolph might well decide to buy the hospital and spend the night."

"You're a swell guy, Feldman. A genuine humanitarian. Go fuck yourself."

He slammed my back door and walked away.

LEAVING THE SORRENTO, I decided to turn in #855 for the day. The hell with it. I'd made a hundred bucks and I was exhausted by the heat and the swamp of emotion. I'd let JJ the mechanic use the extra time to fix the goddamn car. Once and for all. And there was no point in me going back to the hospital, even as a friend to Claire. No point whatsoever. It would only create confusion, and I'd be in the way. But I couldn't stop my mind. It was racing, thinking about her and her mother and our strange connection.

Returning #855 to the taxi barn in Culver City, I pulled into one of the vacant repair stalls. Rap music blared from the shop's inside speakers, and a wall thermometer read ninety-four degrees. JJ was sitting on a bench eating lunch with one of the day drivers. The guy's cab was six feet off the ground on a lift. His ex-cop car taxi looked to be a worse junker than mine.

I walked over to JJ and dropped my keys on the bench. I had to yell above the noise. "It's all yours."

"Now what, motherfucka?"

"The radiator's shot, JJ. The car's been overheating all day."

"Wha'jou expek, babee? It's fuckin' summertime. You should quit the day shiff and go on nights. Motherfuckah runs juss fine at night."

I leaned in close so he could hear me, then handed him a ten-dollar bill. "Do what you can, okay?" I yelled.

"No problema, my man. By the time you get back here tomorrow morning she'll be cool and sweet as fifteen-year-old pussy."

THAT AFTERNOON AND NIGHT in my rubbled apartment,
with time to kill, I turned my phone off and wrote nonstop,
hammering the keys for hours. A sudden blast of energy and
truth. I propped my windows open with the tallest secondhand books I had, to let in the ocean breeze. While I wrote, I
sipped from a six-pack of Cisco wine coolers.

Words spilled out of me like water from a busted main.
Sentences and paragraphs and pages that had been clogged
inside my brain for months, all came gushing out. A good
story, too. Crazy and funny. About two people meeting in an
airport waiting area in a rain delay, getting drunk at the bar,
then screwing in a stall in the ladies room. The guy was a one-
time Vegas blackjack dealer who'd given it up when he found
Jesus. After meeting Linda that night, he changed his mind,
canceled his airline ticket, and told her he'd wait for her until
she got back from Tucson.

By midnight, I had twenty-five pages. I'd thought of Claire
often, but had been so distracted by my story—on such a good
roll—that I kept going.

Exhausted, half-drunk from the sweet wine coolers, I fell
asleep around midnight.

The next day, on the bus on my way to the taxi barn in
Culver City, the newspaper headline was "Tenth Day—Heat
Wave Continues." I reread my story. Even sober and after a
night's sleep, I still liked what I'd written.

It took five minutes to locate #855 in the ocean of yellow
behind the dispatch office. The cab was filthy inside. As usual.
Sergio, the fat fuck, had been true to form.

I felt the hood to test how long the car had been back in the
lot and discovered it was still hot.

Starting the motor, there was no mistaking the sound of
the same radiator hiss. Shitfuck.

I got in, swept the French fries and a McDonald's bag off the passenger seat and drove the half block to the mechanic's shed.

JJ was smiling and the hip-hop music was all but deafening. "Yo, Big Time," he jeered, "what'chu wan firss, the good news or the bad news?"

"My goddamn car's still overheating," I yelled.

At his worktable, JJ flipped a switch that canceled the noise. "Yeah, my brotha, I know. Thaz the bad news."

"Okay," I said, "fucking stab me. Shoot me. What's the good fucking news?"

JJ was sipping coffee. He spat a stream on the engine block of the car he was working on. A puff of steam exploded. "Well . . . " He paused, trying to sound hopeful. "Good news iz I ordered you a radiator. Yours is fucked. Capital F."

"That's not good news!"

"Wait, babee. The new one'll be in today. You're gettin' a rebuilt right outta the factoree. You're my man. I tole you, JJ's watchin' your backside for sure."

"I can't drive that piece of shit. Listen to the fucker. It's hissing already."

"One more day, Bruno. If I'm lyin', I'm dyin'. Just keep the fuckin' A/C off. You'll be okay."

"And what about my goddamn customers? We're in a heat wave."

"Bess I can do, Bru. Sorry, man."

He spent the next twenty minutes running three bottles of stop-leak through my cab's radiator, then let the motor idle so that the sealant would take hold. I was familiar with this procedure. It was the second day in a row I watched it. Except yesterday, there had been three cars ahead of me in the shop.

At dawn it had the look of being another perfect fucking L.A. day. I grabbed two quick fares that morning: one was a house account to the airport and the other was a radio call from UCLA to Topanga Canyon.

Coming back on the Coast Highway, unable to think of anything but Claire, I turned on San Vicente and made my way toward the Sorrento Terrace. It was just after eight o'clock, the start of Marco's shift.

WHEN HE SAW ME and our eyes met, his expression was blank. No smile. Nothing.

Pulling up closer to the entrance, I noticed three guys in white jumpsuits from the building's cleanup crew working on one side of the alcove, hosing down the drive, sweeping up broken glass.

I rolled down the front passenger window. "Hey, Marco, anything good on your board for today?"

He walked around to my side of the car and leaned in. "You didn't hear, right? You don't know?"

"What've you got for me?"

"They're both dead," he said. "Missus Randolph and her daughter."

I felt my stomach tighten. "C'mon, that's crazy. Where'd you hear that?"

"Last night, sometime after ten o'clock. She pushed Sydney off, then she jumped too. Old Mister Abesani in three-oh-one-eight watched the whole thing." Now Marco was pointing. "Look . . ."

I got out of my cab. I walked over and saw the damage for myself. Two cars that had been parked overnight on the side of the building were smashed. One of them, an older Mercedes, had a crushed roof and hood. The other had a huge gouge on the trunk. The windows from both had popped out. Glass remnants and a side mirror were on the ground, being swept up by the work crew.

It was impossible to believe. I turned away.

Marco was behind me. His doorman's hat in his hand, he was running his hands over his face with a handkerchief. "Missus Randolph was forty-two," he said. "Sydney was twenty. A junior at Cal State. What a waste."

I DROVE BACK TO my garage and turned in the cab. No pa-perwork. No explanation. Leaving the keys in the ignition, I walked away.

When I got home, I undressed and took a shower. I was on my bed smoking, still trying to breathe, when I leaned over, clicked on my answering machine, and pressed the REWIND button.

The voice was a woman's, faint and hoarse from crying. There were long pauses. "I got your home number from the doorman ... I ... asked him for it ... Bruno ... I ... I hope you don't mind ...."

Then there was sobbing, and the click of the receiver being hung up.

After that day, I never drove a taxi again.

Photo Remy Boudet

Dan Fante was born in Los Angeles in 1944. At twenty, he quit school and hit the road.

Fante worked as a door-to-door salesman, taxi driver, window-washer, telemarketer, private investigator, hotel night manager, chauffeur, mailroom clerk, deckhand, dishwasher, carnival barker, envelope stuffer, dating-service counselor, furniture salesman, and parking attendant.

Fante's novels, *Chump Change*, *Mooch*, *86'd*, and *Spitting Off Tall Buildings*, comprise a tetralogy about the author's hard-living alter-ego Bruno Dante. His memoir, *Fante: A Family's Legacy of Writing, Drinking, and Surviving*, weaves together the story of his life with that of his father, the novelist and Hollywood screenwriter John Fante. His books have been translated into many foreign languages.

Fante died in 2015.

Printed May 2021 in Quebec, Canada, for the Black Sparrow Press by Marquis. Set in Eames Century Modern with Santa Fe for titling. Interior design by Tammy Ackerman. This first edition has been bound in paper wrappers for the trade.

Black Sparrow Press was founded by John and Barbara Martin in 1966 and continued by them until 2002. The iconic sparrow logo was drawn by Barbara Martin.